Korkoro Boy
and Other Stories

Lara Deguefé

Illustrations by Seifu Abebe

Shama Books

SHAMA BOOKS

A division of Shama p.l.c.
Addis Ababa, Ethiopia

First edition 2005

Published By
SHAMA BOOKS
P.O. Box 8153
Addis Ababa
Ethiopia

Cover Photograph: Biniam Alemu

Printed in Ethiopia by Central Printing Press

CONTENTS

Preface

These short stories are snatches of the everyday lives of children who could get a bang out of life with simple toys they had made with the garbage of the more fortunate and their own imagination; who had to make a living with their labor, at about eight years of age; who didn't go to school because there weren't any or they couldn't pay the fees - and who never thought of complaining.

I have known them all before they became 'people', except one, whose story I learned from fishermen while sitting together on the banks of a river. They will have changed by now but the conditions surrounding them have not. Only others have taken their places.

These are stories of children - children from anywhere. Unreal though they may seem they are real enough to the kids who must live them.

Lara Deguefé

For my grandsons, Taryk and Calin

Korkoro Boy
and Other Stories

I saw them on that hillside, just when I came around a bend. They were all there, laughing and playing with each other. O they were all there - all the kids I had known and others I hadn't but felt I had. Little boys with strange haircuts, some with long hair, some with caps and some with turbans. Little girls with (or without) shawls on their lovely heads. All dressed in whatever clothes - some in rags, some in cast-off shirts, some in gelabyas, some in short shirts which barely covered their bottoms and some in long, homespun garments and some in saris. But all laughing with the bright sunshine on their faces. Amazed I asked:

'What sort of people are you?'

And just as amazed they replied:

'We're not people. We're too little'.

SHADOWS ON THE WADI

Hassan splashed water on his aching head and tried to keep alert a little longer. It would not be much longer. Already the sound of morning could be heard under the creeping light of the desert skies. The isolated voices of migratory birds that had paused for the night in the scattered patches of vegetation not far from the waterhole joined in hesitant conversation.

There was a raucous response from the vulture who followed the wadi and was never far from the cattle and camels and desperate nomads who might not make it to the well.

The sun abruptly chased shadows across the sands. Like all tropical dawns this one was sudden and sweeping. It was day again in this disputed stretch of land between hill country and desert.

It could scarcely have risen over a more desolate place and its shadows were long and stark: shadows of isolated outcrops, half buried in the high dunes on either side of the bare wadi, long dry and waiting for the rains. It cast thick shadows from sparse and solitary clumps of thorn brush. But even though their leaves were gray and heavy with dust, they were harshly beautiful for a passing moment.

The desert is always beautiful in the swift early morning and during the long night. But the days are endless, endurable only to the vulture sitting on a pile of deadwood brought down by the last flood. It greeted the day with indifference.

It was the only kind of day that Hassan could remember. He could have been twelve or thirteen but had never really known. Boys grew up quickly in this frontier region devastated for so many years by border warfare. Now there were only women and children left and scarcely any men, except for the very old.

Hassan's mother had died not far from this wadi, just sitting huddled and motionless and staring at the sand. She had slowly starved. In harsh times mothers went without. With a frail hand she clutched the torn scraps of cloth that had covered her head and body. An empty rice basket and an empty tin mug beside her. The withered traces were nothing but a grotesque shadow on the bare wadi. For a long time after, Hassan had remembered the blue corn beads that still encircled her brown arm. He had finally wandered away and had been taken in by some friendly desert nomads.

The vulture didn't move. It sensed death everywhere but had the time to wait. Its shapeless shadow annoyed Hassan and he longed to shoot the ugly creature but couldn't waste his bullets nor risk betraying himself too openly. He knew well enough were he to weaken and die, the vulture's patience would be rewarded and felt his carnivorous companion was biding his time.

Although only a boy, Hassan knew what life had been like before on this border land. He had heard the old men talk of the days when they could cross the frontier where they wished and follow the rains that provided a scant pasture for their camels and goats. But that was before the people from the hills had chased them away from the only grazing grounds they knew because they had said they didn't belong there. In those days they didn't really know to which country they belonged. It didn't matter. They were nomads and forced to wander for an existence.

They had been a contented people. Their women lithe and beautiful in bright cottons and jewelry, either from their own fashioning or obtained by some fortunate trade. The children were bright-eyed and uncomplaining through their long day chores of herding animals. Their men were dignified and proud of their simple possessions. Today, hardly any men were left. Most of them had been killed and their temporary habitations destroyed by the people from the mountain country.

The nomads had been puzzled by these men from the hills who were now accompanied by pale-skinned foreigners who had strafed their herds and camps, poisoned their waterholes and forced them further into the desert.

There were few wells left for over a million people. This one was in a dried-up wadi. It had been dug by hand with only wooden bowls for digging to a depth of some sixty feet and it was now becoming shallow. Except for nomads and refugees on this side of the frontier, no one was allowed to come here. It was Hassan's duty to shoot without hesitation any stranger he saw lingering near the waterhole. If this one too were poisoned then they all would perish. Hassan was not happy to do this. Didn't the proverbs of his people say that in drought, or any time for that matter, they must share with a stranger? But strangers had become enemies and Hassan had to become a man and deal with such harsh realities.

Today Hassan did not feel like a man. He felt weak and sick and longed for someone to care what became of him. But he must remain alert. Tonight hundreds of nomads would come to the well and he had to cover them. His relief from the main camp would surely arrive before sundown because he was short of food. He had only handfuls of rice left and a little flat bread. However, he knew there was a sickness in the camp and was beginning to wonder if anyone at all could be found to replace him.

On either sides of the wadi were high rocky banks partially covered by dunes and shifting sands. Hassan had found himself a cave gouged out by the fierce torrents of water that swept through the wadi during the heavy rains in the mountains. He didn't mind the the nights except for the cold. He never had enough clothes. He had only a long desert gown and a cloth to protect his head from the sun. During the night, he dared not light a fire for fear of being spotted by the mountain people on the other side of the wadi. And it was at nighttime he had to remain awake. However, the nights are beautiful in the desert. He could almost pluck a star from the sky. They seemed so close to him. But now he shivered and didn't know if he was hot or cold. He went out into the sun and scanned the ridge for some sign of his relief. It must come today or he would be forced to abandon the well and return for food. He couldn't survive for much longer unless the nomads coming tonight could give him a bowl of milk. They always shared what they had but their camels were thin and not giving much milk.

The vulture fluttered awkwardly a little way and then returned to its perch on the dead wood. Hassan ceased his dreaming. It had to be the boy coming from the main camp to relieve him. The nomads were not due till sundown and no stranger would be mad enough to approach the water hole during the day.

He climbed to the top of the dune that covered the cave and again scanned the silent sands. There was no one in sight. He felt disappointed but uneasy. One does not live alone in the desert with only a vulture for company and not sense a new arrival. Then he looked across the wadi and spotted an unfamiliar shadow.

Hassan knew every shadow in the desert; the shadows that moved and those that remained motionless till they shortened away to nothing at mid-day. He had become accustomed to watching shadows before he studied what was causing them.

The shadow was long in the early morning sun and it seemed bulky at the top end. Hassan shifted his gaze to the figure. It was a man from the mountains. He wore a toga and scarcely much else and it was the toga that betrayed him. Desert people don't wear togas; only the men from the cold mountain country were dressed like that. Desert men wore long gowns bound at the waist like his own.

He climbed down swiftly to the cave, hoping that he had not been seen, picked up his rifle and waited.

He didn't need to be alarmed. The figure either had not noticed him nor seemed to care if he had. He walked slowly to the waterhole and did not seem to be aware that the brilliant sunshine revealed him. A wasted dog trailed some paces behind. Hassan waited till the figure was a few paces from the well. He wavered a moment. Who was he and what was he doing there?

He cursed himself for his indecision. One tablet of poison would destroy forever their only source of water. Dazed but determined he fixed an uncertain site on the figure and shot him.

The stranger appeared to have slumped with the sound of the discharge. The dog disappeared behind a thicket but almost immediately returned and crouched beside the still figure on the sand.

Hassan made his way down from the cave and slowly crossed the wadi to the waterhole. The intruder had not moved. He lay on his face, his arms flung out on the side, one hand still clutching an upturned gourd. His thick toga covered his shoulders and part of his head.

Hassan was uneasy. With the butt of his rifle he shoved off the clinging dog and then bent to examine the body for the bullet wound. There was none. He must have missed.

He stood up and stared at the limp form then warily turned it over with his foot. He saw the exhausted beautiful face of a boy who could have been himself - the resemblance was so vivid. He experienced a brief feeling of relief that the stranger must have collapsed from fatigue or thirst before reaching the well. The dog looked at him in reproach then skulked over to the waterhole and gazed pathetically into the depth. There was no way he could reach the water. He came back and crept to the silent body and begged for nothing further.

Hassan was confused and felt a little sick. Why would a mountain youth come to this wadi? Had he been sent to poison it or to spy out the location? He began a complete search. He examined the pockets of the shorts that seemed to be made entirely of patches and found nothing. He took the leather amulet from the Christian boy and shredded it completely. There was nothing in it. The gourd? Taking a stone he smashed it but it was as empty as the desert around him. It was clear that the boy was a wandering victim of the hill country wars. Or was he? The hill people used boys to spy on desert camps.

This inner conflict irritated him. Had he been able to report this or to turn in a captive from beyond the frontier, his own status would have been raised to that of a guerilla fighter and if he did hand him over, he would surely have some information on what they intended to do with the nomads. Hassan was further annoyed by the feeling that he knew that he wasn't going to do this. Didn't the law of the prophet say that you never turned away a stranger from your territory or your well? He drew up a tin of water and splashed it over the frail face of his captive. Still, he would keep him in doubt before he released him this night. Perhaps he could get some information from him. He would at least know some thing about the present condition beyond the border.

It took three tins of water to revive the exhausted boy. The little dog licked the face, the clothes and even the wet sand to moisten his tongue. Hassan was almost collapsing himself from an unusual fatigue.

Samuel opened his eyes and stared at the hostile face of the desert boy.

'What brings you to our wadi and our well?'

'I am in search of water for my mother and my sister and those of our camp.'

'And where is your camp?'

'A day's walking but I got lost. I don't know this country.'

'You come from the mountains where there is plenty of water and you expect me to believe that?'

Samuel sat up and clutched his bare knees defensively:

'We are no longer from the mountains. We lived before near the border town on the side of the escarpment. We were driven from there by our own people and the light-skinned soldiers who are now every where in our country.'

'Why?'

'I don't know,' replied Samuel wearily.

'Where is your father? My authorities would be interested to know.'

' They shot him along with many others and also our cattle. Then they burned our village. We ran away and are camped nearby but we have no water.'

'Are you the man who speaks for your camp?'

'No,' replied Samuel hopelessly, 'I'm not a man. Men are dangerous and if this is what they do to our country then I have no desire to be one. I'm only a boy in search of water for my mother and the children left in the camp. We will die if we don't find water.'

Hassan sat down and faced Samuel. He could no longer remain on his feet and it was becoming hot on the wadi. Samuel stared at Hassan with eyes almost dead with desperation.

'Why did you smash my gourd? How can I return without water for the journey?'

'I was searching for the poison you brought to destroy our well.' persisted Hassan.

'I bring no poison,' repeated Samuel evenly, 'why would I poison the water I need to drink? I have told you I search only water and people who will share with us. We are not many and have no livestock.'

Hassan rose uncertainly. 'Come with me till I decide what to do with you. My relief is coming soon. Together we shall discuss it.'

'May I have water to drink?' pleaded Samuel, 'and also for my dog?'

'A dog shall not drink from my water can.'

'Why not?' asked Samuel stubbornly, 'A camel does. What is so different between a thirsty camel and thirsty dog?'

'A camel provides milk and meat and hide. A dog is good for nothing.'

'He is my friend! He is some one to talk to. Don't you ever need someone to talk to in your lonely post that you share with a vulture? Does it not also drink from your well? Give me water and my dog shall drink from the palm of my hand.'

Hassan's headache aggravated him and he was angry with himself for being so inhospitable and mean to this stranger. He drew more water and poured it into Samuel's cupped hands who in turn gave it to the dog.

They climbed the hill in silence to the cave.

Hassan shared a handful of cooked rice and a piece of dried flat bread with his captive. Samuel shared his portion with the dog who waited outside the cave. They ate without speaking. Hassan's thoughts tormented him. Should he release this boy now or wait till his relief came? If what he said were true he would not be able to travel by day anyway. And how could he travel without water? Hassan felt guilty. He had smashed Samuel's gourd and he hadn't another container of any kind to give him. He had only a jerry can with which he drew water and a dipper fashioned from a gourd. He had found a small cavern in the cave that was watertight and this he kept filled for emergencies. But now his reason became more and more confused and his head ached unbearably. He would let Samuel go tonight after the nomads had left. But should he give him permission for his people to shift camp closer to the wadi? That, he would decide during the day. Or was it better to wait till his relief came and consult with him? He didn't even know if he would come today and there was little left to eat for two. He couldn't remain awake indefinitely to guard him. He sat with his rifle ready and tried to think through his aching head and shivering body.

Despite his exhausting journey, Samuel was alert enough. A little food and water had revived him. It seemed that Hassan would insist that he had been sent to spy out the water hole. If Hassan's relief believed that the nomads would be strafed by men from his own country, then he would never get away. He and his dog would probably be shot. He watched Hassan closely and knew that the boy couldn't remain awake that night.

The vulture never moved and its shadow now began to lengthen. The day seemed endless. Samuel covered himself with his toga and decided to sleep. He would need the strength.

He awoke to a great clamor of voices. It was evening and the nomads had come.

Dozens of camels and many women and children crowded around the well and seemed to fill the wadi. They drew up water in old cans, gourds and wooden basins while Hassan covered them from the dune above the cave.

The women milked the camels and brought up a wooden basin of milk to Hassan who was still outside the cave. Then they loaded their water containers onto their camels and started back to their sparse pastures. The water level in the well was now low but it would seep in again during the night. The boys drank some milk and left a little to curdle for tomorrow. Samuel dozed again while the dog searched hopelessly for some remains of food beside the water hole.

Was he dreaming or was Hassan talking? Someone must have come. He lay in the dark and listened and looked around the cave. No one else was there but the voice of Hassan grew louder. Samuel sat up abruptly and realized that Hassan was raving. He talked endlessly but he wasn't talking to Samuel. He had let go of his rifle which was lying on the floor of the cave. He shivered and muttered words that made no sense. Samuel leaned over and watched him and then got up quickly and moved the rifle beyond his reach. He squatted beside him and touched his body. It was dry and hot. Hassan had desert fever. Samuel knew because dozens of children in his camp had died from it. Sometimes they became covered with red spots and sometime they just died from the fever.

He covered him with his toga and then looked down at the well where his dog was still searching in the muddy tracks. A full moon was rising and there were uncertain shadows on the wadi. He could get away in the night but must leave more water for Hassan. Going cautiously down to the water hole he drew up a jerry can of water and struggled up the hill to the cave. The level of the water was low but hopefully the rains would soon come and there would be plenty. If only he had been given permission to return and share the well!

Hassan still lay on the floor muttering strange words about his mother. Samuel thought of his own, waiting and wondering if he had gotten lost or attacked by animals or men.

Then Samuel saw the vulture in the moonlight, sweeping low over the wadi and back and forth over the cave. Did that loathsome creature never sleep? The vulture hadn't eaten and was sensing already where its next meal would be. It returned and perched on the dead tree, its shadow a shapeless, sinister blotch on the sand. Samuel well knew that vultures, like hyenas in his own hill country, did not always wait for someone to die. They followed anything that was too weak to walk and there was no stockade he could build against a vulture.

Hassan kept talking and Samuel kept covering him again with his toga. They would have to sleep side by side for the rest of this night as that was the only cover they had. He lay down beside Hassan and the two boys slept. Soon, the little dog crept in beside them.

The sun rose again on the wadi and Samuel waited.

He waited three days. He kept Hassan's fever down by continually splashing his body with water and forcing him to drink. During the night the two boys and the dog continued to sleep under the toga but even the dog was so thin it didn't supply much warmth. When the mornings came, Samuel and the dog lay out in the sun to warm themselves after the bitter cold of the night. Samuel fed Hassan the curdles of milk and he and the dog ate the rest of the bread.

On the third evening, Hassan no longer shook but was cooler and slept quietly. Samuel had to go or risk being killed. The nomads would be returning to the well and Hassan's relief could come at any time. He would leave water and the last few grains of rice in the cave.

He no longer thought much about how he himself was going to exist without water for the journey. He had to go.

He felt uneasy. Except for the vulture and the dog and Hassan, he was alone in the wadi. But he didn't feel alone. He felt watched and even the dog kept stirring, sniffing at the entrance of the cave and looking back at Samuel with a question in his eyes. Perhaps he was anxious to leave this place where he sensed he didn't belong.

Hassan's fever had now left him and he showed signs of waking. Why did the vulture keep fussing? There must be someone else around the wadi or was that horrible bird waiting for them all to die? Samuel had to leave after sundown. He would have to return to the camp and then scout for another source of water. And he would have to travel without water as Hassan's dipper was useless for a journey. He would drink well before he left and try not to get lost again.

He examined the rifle before placing it beside Hassan. He had never even held one let alone fired it. It was old and heavy and still loaded. Samuel shuddered when he remembered that one of those bullets could have killed him.

He placed the rifle and the can of water beside the sleeping Hassan. His toga he had to take so he covered the boy with the ragged pieces of cloth he had used for his turban. It was with reluctance he prepared to leave without permission to return. Neither could he risk his life by remaining any longer. He had to report to the people in the camp that there was no water for them here.

The moon was full and moonlight on the desert can be beautiful if you have water and food and hope in your heart. Samuel had none of these. He paused a moment to look at the shadow patterns on the wadi.

A complaining croak from the vulture ripped the silence around him. The ugly bird moved from his dead tree to a thornbush not very far away. Samuel clamped a hand over the dog's muzzle and momentarily froze. Someone had come to the wadi. He waited in silence as he saw two men approach the waterhole.

Samuel shook with violence. He had seen these kind of men before. They were not even his own people but worked with them--light skinned mercenaries and dressed in green khaki. It was men like these who had killed his father and burned their huts. Had they come for water or to poison the well?

He trembled with terror and disgust. He didn't even know if he feared more for himself or for the well. What would Hassan's relief do to him if he found him here? What would those mercenaries do if they found him in the cave? And what would the nomads do if their only source of water was poisoned?

He had no choice. The men strolled leisurely towards the well. They didn't seem to be in a hurry. They chattered and laughed in a language that Samuel had heard before but didn't understand. Then they stopped, stretched out on the sand, ate from some food in their packs and drank from shiny water canteens that glinted in the moonlight.

Samuel took up Hassan's rifle. He scarcely knew what to do with it. He released the safety catch and drew a dusty hand over his dry mouth. What if he missed? Those men would be well armed.

It seemed an hour of slow minutes before they got up and started for the well and it seemed minutes of slow seconds before he had the courage to raise the rifle. The two men swayed before his eyes as he fired twice. And it seemed to Samuel that he heard the shots before he fired them. How many times had he fired? He couldn't remember. He thought that he'd heard shots from all around him. Perhaps he too had desert fever like Hassan. He staggered to his feet from where he had been thrown by the sudden discharge of the heavy rifle. He must be alone on the wadi. Even the vulture had taken off for the moment. He cleared his eyes and stared and stared. The two men lay slumped on the sand.

Samuel waited a long time with the shaking dog pressed beside him. He had to be certain that the two men were dead. He waited for what seemed to be hours but wasn't really very long. Then he climbed down very slowly from the embankment and crossed the wadi, the little dog following uneasily behind.

Timidly he approached the two bodies, crumpled and staring in the moonlight. They were well clothed and well fed. Their faces were the light skinned faces of foreigners. He prodded the bodies with the butt of his rifle and found them inert and heavy and stared a long time at their lifeless faces.

He knelt and unstrapped their pistols and belts of ammunition and then cut loose their water canteens. They were half full so they had not traveled far by foot. Indeed, their dead faces didn't even look weary. He cautiously poured out the water and then searched the packs on their backs. He found strange little boxes and bottles that he couldn't understand. Were they food, medicine or were they poison? The writing was different. Samuel could read his own language but this was certainly not his own. There were chunks of brown bread and that he could understand. He set them aside to tie later in a piece of cloth for his return journey. Then he examined again the boxes of tablets and noticed a small picture on the outside. It was a picture of a face with no skin, just bones and holes where the eyes had been. He had seen these bodies often enough on the edges of the camps and scattered around the countryside and decided they must be poison for the well. What was he going to do with them? He couldn't leave them on the bodies. Soon women and children would come to the well and thinking they were medicine would take them. He didn't want to take them with him for fear he might be caught. Bury them in the bed of the wadi? No! The rains were coming and there would be flash floods sweeping wide and deep and then the water would be polluted. He would have to take them and throw them away somewhere on his return journey. He wrapped them carefully in a cloth and put them aside. He looked at the clothes the dead men wore and shuddered with disgust and loathing. He didn't want them. However, he removed a belt from one of the soldiers. Samuel had never owned a belt; his shorts were always tied with a piece of string. The belt was too large but he wrapped it around him twice. He unstrapped a pack; that he could use. Then he filled the two canteens with water from the well and gathering his treasures and the boxes of poison, he climbed back to the cave.

He put a canteen of water and some bread beside the still sleeping Hassan and left the rifle within his reach. The two pistols and ammunition he left in the cave. Of what use were they in a defenseless camp? Then, strapping a canteen of water on his hip, he arranged his toga over his shoulder, picked up his cloth of bread and with the little dog crossed the wadi for the last time.

He passed the bodies of the two dead mercenaries. They wouldn't be there for long. Already the vulture had been joined by some friends. Samuel climbed the slope on the wadi and turned for a last look at the cave and his bare feet froze in the still warm sand!

Standing on the dune above the cave stood a tall desert tribesman, his white gowned figure casting the longest moonlight shadow Samuel had ever seen. He leaned casually on his rifle and did not seem to be concerned by the presence of a hill country boy near the waterhole.

Hassan's relief had come. For how long had he been there? How long had he been watching him? Perhaps throughout the whole day.

How could Samuel ever have dreamed that it had been himself who had shot those soldiers and what would that man do to him when he found those pellets of poison in his sack?

Should he attempt to explain or would he even be given the chance?

A long moment passed. Samuel was unable to move. Was he playing with him? It would not be difficult for such a marksman. And then the tall figure waved his hand in the desert signal to go in peace and the salute meant that the waterhole was a symbol of friendship between them.

Samuel returned the salute, then turned a happy face towards the distant blocks of granite that covered the land between the desert and the mountains and the long and dangerous journey to the cruel miseries of his camp. The small dog, yearning for its harsh but familiar surroundings ran before him.

Two little shadows followed them till the moon rose higher and both shadows disappeared in the sand and rocks and thorn brush which extended for miles into the foothills.

THE KASHMIRI RUG

Pati could scarcely see the pattern of the green leaves she was embroidering. She must get them done, and exactly. That was her job - to do all the green leaves, the leaves of that tree which grows only in Kashmir. And they had so many points on them for weary little fingers. And there wasn't much time as she had to complete half a rug a day. The white Kashmir rug, made from the wool of the goats, which ranged the hills and couldn't care less what happened to their wool, was thick and heavy for small fingers and those pointed leaves had to be exact.

There was no time for tears. Tears that stung her eyes - or were they tears? She blinked to squeeze them out but they kept coming. She picked up the edge of her soiled sari and furtively wiped them away. She can't have fatigued eyes and hoped the master wouldn't notice in the dim attic with its sloping roof and only one small dirty window. Even when they cleaned it, it didn't give much light. But she must be swift and accurate to earn one anna by nightfall. Why were her flashing black eyes so bleary today? It must be the tears, she thought, and continued to blink them away.

The master had slashed Pati with a bamboo branch because the memsahib had not bought any Kashmiri rugs. It was she who had brought the memsahib to the factory.

Yesterday night, she had been sitting on the board steps of one of those matchbox houses one finds only in Srinagar along the banks of the Jammu River. She had crept in there to find refuge from the heavy monsoon rain. She thought all houses in the world were like that because her small world was only Srinagar. When the house was not big enough, they would build another layer on top till they all looked like they would topple into the river but never did - at least not in her nine years.

All the houses in the town had been built by the river because there was only one road and if people wanted to go anywhere, they had to take a shakira. A shakira was a small boat with a canopied place at one end. Small boys would pole or paddle for a few rupees to where you wanted to go. But Pati never took a shakira because she didn't have any rupees. She got up at four every morning and walked the long way around the river and passed over a shaky, swinging plank bridge to where there was another toppling house.

There, she scurried up to the attic where children worked on the mats. The bottom floor was much grander than the creaking old attic because that was where the master displayed the finished rugs but none of the children were allowed in there. The master had a nasty temper and could get very angry if he didn't have enough customers.

But now, a lot of ladies were climbing that shaky old stairway where Pati was sitting. They must be foreign people as a plane had come in that day. Anyway, she knew from their clothes and their excited voices that they were not from the town. She huddled closer to the wall of the rough stairway with her baby sister on her knees to let them pass. That was her other job, minding her sister while her mother made curried vegetables over the fire. It seemed that the old merchant up top was going to do a lot of business that night. O he would say - not for buying; just for looking! And he would offer them spiced tea and soon a small servant would come running down the stairs to get it. And they would all be there a long time because they looked like they would do a lot of buying. She listened to their excited chatter:

'I want some Kashmiri material. They say it's the real stuff from those goats on the mountains.'

'I want to find some jade and tiger-eye gems. They say it's from Tibet.'

'I want some wood carvings and some of those brass bells and leg ornaments. They're so different.'

'Isn't this the quaintest place! And those little shakiras!'

'Are you staying on a houseboat?'

'O No! They're not clean, you know. We're staying at the big hotel. It's so modern for a place like this!'

'Well, I only want a Kashmiri rug. You know those lovely white ones made from the wool of the goats on the hillside and embroidered with pink and red flowers surrounded by a trellis of green leaves. I know exactly where I'm going to put it.'

'O yes! They're so unique and one finds them nowhere else in the world. In fact, for a good price, I might buy ten and have them shipped home. They would make such marvelous wedding presents.'

Ignoring Pati, they rushed past like the waters of the river from the mountains in the spring. Except the last memsahib. She noticed Pati on the stairway and stopped and said kindly, 'Hello, little one.'

How were they going to carry all those things, she wondered, and how did they have the money to pay for them all? And what would they do with all those rugs? Did they sleep on them? She did but not on Kashmiri rugs. There were only three or four mats in her mother's hut and they were made of river grass. For certain, they had plenty of money and would not realize how much that old merchant above was going to cheat them. He paid little for all those piles of goods he had up there. She had often seen him sitting in his shakira and haggling with little boys when they emptied their sacks of collected objects around him. He was even meaner than the master she worked for all day and he was mean enough. But he did sell his rugs for less and the merchant above hated him and never told the outside people about him. Her master would tell all the children in the attic to tell everyone where they could find a Kashmiri rug for less rupees and then perhaps, he would give them a few annas extra. But the children never did.

They were too occupied in playing or fetching water at night and what was so wonderful about a rug anyway? Didn't they get dirty? Or perhaps the people with shoes didn't get mats dirty. Perhaps they could walk on them and they still didn't get dirty.

She found a piece of chapatti in the folds of her sari, tore half of it into small pieces for the baby and ate the rest herself while thinking of the vegetable curry her mother and other mothers would be stewing in those big iron pots on the common fire of dung outside their bamboo huts. She had to keep the baby away till sunset.

Pati became tired of sitting crouched on the steps. She sat all day in the attic and her young bones ached for stretching. She placed the baby on a step and played a game with herself running up and down the stairs, pausing at the top to listen to the voices inside.

'I do want that anklet. It must be a hundred years old!'

'... and this! I must have it!'

They must be stupid, these outside people. Didn't they know that if you wanted anything, you must pretend you didn't want it? Else the merchant's calculating eyes would notice and he would double the price and who wants something that's a hundred years old anyway.

Pati looked at her brown bare feet with the blue plastic bangle circling her slim ankle. Who would want one a hundred years old? It would be heavy and ugly and with this one, she could buy another for one anna. It was the only decoration she had except for her lovely face and dark tresses. She would have to wait till her marriage when perhaps her future husband would buy her gold. The ladies were coming out and she hurried back to the steps and the baby.

They had indeed bought a lot. They had so many parcels they could hardly squeeze past her where she crouched on the stairway unnoticed.

'I wonder how long it's going to take for those ten Kashmiri rugs to get to America--if they get there at all. He said ten weeks but you can never trust these people. And you didn't even buy one?'

'I didn't quite like the needlework on any and many were soiled,' remarked the lady who had noticed her on the stairway, 'and I must say he didn't come down much on the price you paid for ten.'

'O I don't care! They're so exotic and different and my friends won't notice the marks I am sure!'

'But I only wanted one for myself and I didn't really like the way the pattern was finished.' And they trudged down the darkening passage.

'Memsahib,' Pati heard herself calling. She dumped the baby and stood up. 'I know where you can find a beautiful Kashmiri rug. Beautiful and cheaper.'

The memsahib paused and turned back. She seemed to have forgotten Pati in her disappointment.

'But how would you know?' she asked in amazement.

'I...Well...I just know,' Pati fumbled, 'but you would have to take a shakira.' She stopped and wondered if the memsahib had enough rupees and it was dark now.

'You can show me tomorrow. I'll meet you here at ten in the morning.'

'O...not here,' Pati faltered, '... upstream by the riverside and it would have to be at five...' she added hopefully,' the early morning light is so pretty and the river is not so crowded.'

She twisted her hands and shied away. Her green leaves were so neatly done and she never got the white mat dirty while working. But would such a grand memsahib get up at five just with the sun? And their mats were spotless and well embroidered with carefully chosen colours. The master saw to that.

The memsahib was either amused or interested. Pati trembled. She had never spoken to such a grand lady before. But would she be there? If not, then she would have to run and run all the way around the river to be at work on time. The memsahib promised she would be there.

She was and it was a lovely ride by shakira with the morning light picking out one by one the half-opened lotuses that floated on the lake once they passed beyond the river. Pati sat in the stern with the paddle boy and the memsahib on the cushions in the canopied section.

The master was already leaning on the wooden sides of the swinging bridge and counting the small heads of his staff who hurried without a greeting immediately to the attic. He was a handsome creature in his white gelabya and embroidered skullcap covering the head of his bearded face and he was conscious of it all. He was amazed seeing Pati arrive for work by shakira followed by a memsahib. His sharp eyes noticed a customer and he made a big show of Pati, patting her head and pulling her towards him.

She pulled away from his unaccustomed advances and fled to the attic leaving him to show his rugs to the lady.

'The child told me you make Kashmiri rugs?'

'Indeed I do, Madame. The best in Srinagar.' And dashing into the shack he selected the best - his showpiece - and held it stretched out before her. 'No need to buy. Just for looking.'

It was such a beautiful rug made from the felt of the angora mountain goats. He had wanted to sell that one for a long, long time. White, so white and embroidered with such intricate patterns worked by tiny fingers. He followed the lady's interest with keen eyes.

'It's almost what I wanted and certainly much better than in the village,' she considered slowly, 'how much?'

'No need to discuss it now,' he insisted, 'come and have some spiced tea and simets. It's early for you,

Madame.' He had ascertained her interest already. She was not the showy type but she had money as he noted from her large camera equipment.

'No,' she replied, 'I haven't much time. I have to leave for Delhi at two this afternoon. How much?'

Seeing a possible loss in bargaining over the usual hospitality he grabbed what seemed a fading opportunity.

'Madame, before we discuss the price, will you do something for me? Will you take a picture of me holding your rug? It will be your rug. I want to show the picture in the big hotel so everyone will come to my shop where the best rugs are made.'

Taking a picture is a small favour to ask an American. She took several of him, standing in his white garments offset by his black beard and light brown skin and leaning on the railing of the bridge, holding her rug and only a few feet from the blue water of the river with full blown lotus flowers. It made a charming picture.

'And now I would like to photograph your women at their work. I would like to see the weave of their looms.'

'With pleasure, Madame,' he beamed and together they climbed the stairs to the attic. It was dim to begin with and even with the later sun, it would not be much else. There were no looms and there were no women. Just twenty small dark heads bending fearfully over piles of embroidery on which there seemed to be endless bright patterns and their brightness was all that added a little radiance to the attic. Some had chairs, others had only benches which were too low to reach the table and so they had to kneel on them. There was no laughter and no childish chatter. Everyone worked with a prolonged frenzy and the memsahib wasn't kind and polite anymore. In fact she looked as horrified as if a black cobra had crawled over her foot.

·

She took a picture and they were so proud to be photographed, straining their pinched faces to reach the camera with the master beaming behind them and so pleased with himself. But not for long.

The memsahib didn't buy the rug.

COOKY

Her face was like an oven baked gingerbread cookie. A cookie's face never changes once out of the oven. Cooky's didn't either. It was round with straight, black, short banged hair and was forever so. And as for being gingerbread - her mother was an Indian and her father a metis (person of mixed blood), all of which made Cooky a gingerbread indeed. Black raisin eyes, a painted smile and a round face. That was Cooky and that was all she had to present to the world around her. If she got upset or excited, her expression never changed and no one had ever seen her cry and she never forgot anything either. Cooky, like a cookie, was complete.

The teacher would arrive in the morning apprehensive of the forty changing faces before her, faces of many changes and many temperaments. Some impassive - those were the Indians. But they weren't many, as they had little chance to attend a mixed school. Some soft and friendly - those were the metis; some hard and daring - those were the debris of Europe, whose parents had drifted to the derelict and now fishing and trapping community of this northern Canadian village. But Cooky was a constant. She was there every morning sitting at her desk and watching her intently with that same, same smile. With the others, all depended on the night they had spent before, the teacher realized that she had to be sympathetic for this was a wild and unruly place where children weren't considered over much,

'Eric,' she had once asked a thin, wasted Swedish boy of seven years, 'where did you get that cut on your face?'

'I was so damn drunk, Teacher, I fell in the wood box.'

But this is Cooky's story.

Cooky's father was the owner of the only grocery shop in the village. A shack in the old form of years ago, with two running counters on either side and the shelves behind stacked high with basic provisions which, if one was lucky, were generally available but depended on the last lake barge in the village. He was a metis with only one functioning eye, the other probably having been lost in a drunken brawl which were common evening occurrences in the village, being remote and outside of whatever law overlooked liquor controls. He was over-charming and sly and no doubt corrupt within the measures available to him. His wife was a fat, illiterate, amiable Indian who could rise to the occasion whenever the teacher had to come to their house. Which was seldom, but he, being the chairman of the school board, had to be handled from time to time. There, she would be offered tea in chipped cups with no matching saucers and could imagine the pottery-throwing rows, which were no doubt all too frequent.

Cooky's face fascinated her although she knew that Cooky felt she favored Gladys and Patsy more. She tried not to have any favorites, but some kids are just more naturally responsive and appealing than others. But Cooky was impressive and the teacher found her intriguing. Every time she looked up, it was Cooky's face she saw first and she longed to know what was behind that painted smile. Was there loneliness in her house? She could imagine there was. Her parents were kind enough to her when they were sober but that wasn't often. Did anyone ever cuddle her, talk to her? Did she ever giggle over some childish prank? She must be a desolate child behind it all but with a brave defiance to her small outside world.

She was bright enough. Often the teacher would notice her sitting and doing nothing - just watching her.

'Cooky! Get working! Finish your sums.'

'I've finished, Teacher'. And they were always correct.

'If you're that smart, I'd better promote you to grade two.' But she knew she couldn't. Those were the old days of education in a small village where a child, although bright, couldn't be promoted within a year. At least not without a jabbing jealousy which would arise from the whole community and make the kid's life miserable. Anyway, why hurry? They had no future and usually dropped out of school at fourteen to be of greater use elsewhere.

'Cooky? What did you do last.night?'

'I did my homework, Teacher.'

'But Cooky! You are only six. You have no homework.'

No reply. Only black, impassive eyes with just a hint of adoration.

A different kind of adoration than that of her sister, Anna, who was already ten and not bright at all but used her wiles to get consideration. The teacher got impatient with her and with the two boys. She had four of that family in school, and they were all a neglected bunch. She could tell. Their lunch was always store stuff - dry biscuits and fish scraps. Adequate enough compared to many, but crude. Most of the children were poor, enjoying occasional treats when the catch of fish or fur was abundant but with no continuity in their lives. She hoped the children felt they at least belonged somewhere when at school.

She did some asking and learned that Cooky had been born on a barge one night crossing the lake. She had been tossed on a pile of raw skins collected en route, as her drunken mother hadn't even realized she had given birth. And there Cooky remained till the woman came out of it and gave her milk.

'Cooky, do you have a doll to play with?' the teacher asked her one day.

'No. I had once but I don't like dolls because they don't say anything. They just look and their faces are always the same. I have a cat.' The teacher knew the cat because Cooky brought it every day to school.

Sometimes she carried it and sometimes it just followed slowly behind. She must have started out early to school because she and the cat were never late.

It was a no-account cat, dirty - white with orange and black spots scattered wherever and had the same expression as Cooky. A sort of serene and everlasting smile. The teacher got used to it sitting on the windowsill in the sun of winter and summer during class. At recess Cooky would play with it and no one ever teased or touched that cat.

There must have been some inner fury behind Cooky's enigmatic smile. The cat was well-fed because, after all, this was a fishing village. After school finished at four it followed Cooky home.

'Cooky,' said the teacher one cold winter recess when Cooky had remained because she had a sore throat, 'would you like me to read you a story?'

'No,' replied Cooky, her moon face just reaching over the top of the teacher's desk, 'TELL it!'

'Why? What is the difference? A book has pictures.'

'Because when you TELL a story your face has more pictures than the book and you sound more like the animals.'

'The animals?'

'Yes. I want the stories of the animals.'

'Why?'

'Because your animals are so smart. The little red hen can make bread. Our hens can't do that. The three little pigs make houses. I have never seen pigs build a house and your wolves dress up in grandma's clothes.'

It was clear that Cooky wasn't going to make a trapper's wife. The teacher shoved her homework aside.

'I see. Well, which one do you want me to TELL?'

'The gingham dog and the calico cat because they eat each other up!'

Cooky had a relish in her voice and no doubt wished her parents would do the same and thus conclude the family rows in the house.

She listened intently and then asked: 'Teacher, is my cat a calico?'

'Well, sort of. Yes, she's calico.'

'Now, the one about the owl and the pussy cat.' Cooky knew all about owls. There were plenty abroad during the northern nights.

'Teacher, do you think my cat will marry an owl and go over the lake in a green boat?'

'Well, I don't know,' hesitated the teacher, caught out of fancy, 'do you want her to marry an owl?'

'No. I want her to stay home with me. And now, the little red....'

'Cooky,' reminded the teacher, 'recess is over and you may go out and ring the bell.'

Cooky hoisted the bell which was half as big as herself and shook it furiously at the door.

Her sore throat didn't seem to heal very quickly for she remained in at recess a week. Patsy and Gladys might be more winsome and persuasive in class but the teacher began to feel that by her cunning determination, Cooky had adopted her.

One day Cooky was not in school which the teacher found unusual.

The Barette kids, all four of them, were always there. Cooky's cat, which had begun to look a little too well-fed, had disappeared and Cooky, without saying anything to her parents, who probably weren't there in any case, had gone to search for it. It was winter and she finally found it buried under the snow like the smart huskies did to keep warm on winter nights. But she had produced seven kittens and they were all frozen, the cat not realizing that she could keep her own body warm under the snow but not seven others. She didn't want to leave her frozen family so Cooky, well-dressed in parka and mukluks (sealskin high boots), stayed with the cat. What words of comfort they gave each other in that cold snowy night no one ever knew because Cooky didn't say anything to anyone. She just arrived home early next morning with her half-dead cat inside her parka and was herself put to bed as she was also severely frost bitten. A week later, she was back at school but without her cat. Apparently it had not survived for long. If Cooky suffered any loss, she didn't show it. There were no tears in her opaque black eyes and no sadness on her small brown face.

The teacher, when she had the time would call her up to her desk and help her catch up on last week's lessons but had no way of knowing if the child was hurting inside for Cooky just thanked her with that forever smile.

The teacher was leaving. It was talked about at recess that she was joining up to help fight a war. Cooky didn't know about any war except the ones that perpetually raged in her own home. All she knew was that the teacher was going away and that some were sorry and some, the wild rabble, didn't care. During that last, week there was no organized effort to give her a proper send-off. Some gave her little trinkets probably out of a popcorn box and with tearful partings. Gladys and Patsy had put together ninety cents and had given her a plastic case with writing paper inside and one boy gave her a pair of beaded moccasins his mother had made.

Early next morning, she went to the schoolhouse to clear her desk. A window was open, which shouldn't have been. On her desk was a bunch of half-wilted flowers with a piece of page torn out of an exercise book on which was carefully printed,

'Goodbye Teacher.'

She kept that scrap of paper for a long, long time till it faded and got lost as memories do.

LIMPOPO

It was the stranger who first noticed the basket by the side of the road. The colours were such a beautiful blend of meadow and sky. He almost drove past it. But braked and reversed to where it was placed alone on a plain tan mat that didn't interfere with it. It seemed to say, 'look at me - only me.' Whoever had arranged that display was indeed an artist.

Beside it, on another mat, lay a young boy, a cripple with a cane nearby. A small no-account but defiant dog shared his mat. The stranger got out and examined the basket. The fiber and dyes were carefully chosen and it was well finished both inside and out. Thinking the boy's mother had made it, he said:

'How much does your mother ask for this? I want to buy it.'

'My mother didn't make it. She works in the fields and has no time for weaving. It's my basket. I made it myself.'

'YOU made it? That's usually women's work.'

The boy winced slightly and looked away. The man, wishing he hadn't said that, added hastily, 'Well, how much do YOU want for it?'

'I don't know.'

'You don't KNOW?' the stranger sat down beside the basket and looked around him at the cluster of small huts behind. It was a poor village and he could see no handicraft shop so asked, ' How much are baskets around here?'

'I don't know. I've just finished making it. It's the first one I've ever made. I never thought of selling it.'

'Why?'

'I like to look at it. It tells a story. A story of a happy place where I used to work long ago.'

The stranger took a long look at the boy. His hip was almost gone and what was left of it trailed a mangled leg. It can't have been so very long since you were born, he mused to himself, and if you were born like that then I can't imagine you working any place. Aloud, he said, 'I'll pay you well for it. In fact, I'd like many. Anyone who can make a basket like this can make another and more. You must know the story it tells?'

'Yes.'

'What is it about?'

'Me.'

'Tell me.'

So the boy told him an incredible tale. He told it like the tellers-of-tales do. Faraway from himself:

Kunaynee was idle and pestered by the flies. He lay on his back and chewed a small stick of sugar cane that someone from the nearby plantation had given him. It was well past noon on the lower reaches of the tropical plateau and the hottest hour of the day. The cattle needed no tending. He had taken them to the river to water early in the morning and was not concerned about them. They stood, melancholy and motionless beneath the shade of a few sparsely scattered acacia trees. So pressed together were they that it was doubtful if they got any relief at all from the sun by being in the shade. There was not even a little wind to chase away the flies and the birds that sat on their backs to feed on the insects. Even they had fled to cooler places.

Kunaynee thought about the river - Limpopo. It was not a beautiful river. It was grey and muddy because of the soil it carried and at this time of the year it moved slowly. He had never, ever, seen blue water. Even when the river was wild and swift it was still the color of the hippo and the crocodile who lived in it. An endless grey reptile cutting through the plateau and attempting to reach the sea.

But to Kunaynee, it was beautiful and fascinating. There were trees that hung low over its water. Monkeys swung from those trees, wild boars grunted through the underbrush and birds built hanging nests everywhere.

Many people hated the river because of the lives lost to the crocodiles. But what is a village without a river? And for as long as they could remember it had been called the Limpopo - the Crocodile River. And the Limpopo was creepy with crocs.

Just never, ever trust a crocodile, he had been told. It's not for nothing they have no friends except the hippo and they tolerate them only because they're useful. They keep the river weeds down so the limpopos can find their prey more quickly. The crocs will not attack a hippo because their skin is too tough and anyway, the hippos are large and fierce enough to be let alone and they are not interested in crocs as they themselves are vegetarians. So they

exist together mutually in useful tolerance of each other
and the hippos keep the crocs in their place. But the crocodiles are sneaky and don't always keep to their place.
They will sometimes attack unsuspecting elephants (not
often) while they are drinking because their trunks are
spreadout over the water and trunks are tender and the
crocodiles know this. The elephants come in herds and a
herd of elephants coming to drink or bathe just takes over
the whole river for itself. They can squash a croc with one
foot and frequently do. So the crocs, the hippos and the
elephants put up with one another and Kunaynee kept out
of the way of them all.

The river was a good mile away but for a highland
boy that was a short walk. He would go down and put just
his head in the water and dampen his homespun shirt. He
knew he couldn't go into the water. He was a grown lad
of nine and knew all about the dangers there.

Many children, he knew were swept in by the power-
ful tail of the crocodile whose slit eyes could scarcely be
seen above the level of the water. The children would be
warned but they were just so little to be fetching water.
Struggling with the weight of large earthen pots they
often stumbled and fell into the edge of the river. That
would be enough. They would never be seen again. An
overturned waterpot caught in the reeds being the only
explanation of their failure to return. But Kunaynee was
a shepherd. He didn't fetch water as that was women's
work. He helped his father with the animals and thought
long thoughts about what he'd do when he grew up.

Sometimes the idea of having his own kraal (enclo-
sure for domestic animals) and a few cows didn't interest
him much. Like many little African shepherds, he was by
nature an artist and a thinker because he lived with the
countryside all day and every day and had nothing else to
do but chase cows around for better pasture. However his
future was fixed and so he didn't question it.

He was relieved to reach the river, now low and slug-
gish as it was the season just before the rains. He scanned
the surface and saw only the barely protruding ears of a
lone hippo basking in the shallows on the opposite side.
He squatted on the large flat stone where his mother did

the washing for the family and plunged his head many
times into the tepid water. After splashing himself all
over, he sat for a long time flipping his dusty bare feet in
and out of the shallow pool around the stone.

The days end quickly in the tropics and Kunaynee
became aware that he had been away from the cattle too
long. It would be a longer hike back to the highland
meadow. Still, he wanted to wait till at least one monkey
came out to tease him and a few birds began to skim the
water. It was so quiet − too quiet. Kunaynee had not
noticed that he was being watched for some time.

He had to go. Without even scanning the surface again
he dunked his head for one last time in the water around
the stone and felt a blow of blackness and then felt nothing more.

Kunaynee was dreaming the languid dreams of men
under water. But he wasn't under water. He put out his
hand and felt rock and dry mud. The movement caused
him pain and a wet sensation on his back and legs. He
blinked but couldn't see except for something like charcoal flames in the darkness before his eyes. He thought
he must be dead and lost consciousness again.

How long it was he didn't know, but he suddenly felt
himself alive again. This time with horror. A cold, thudding shove against his nearly numb legs chilled him to a
shaking alertness. The long, slimy snout of a crocodile
was prodding his body.

He wasn't dead after all but someone wanted him
dead! Crocodiles, well he knew, have no chewing teeth
and prefer their lunch rotten and soft. As was their custom, the wiley old croc had dragged him down the river
and shoved him into this shaft-like river cave to decay
while returning to inspect the body from time to time. He
made a painful attempt to see and realized he was in a
river cave, open at the top, like an abandoned well. He
tried to move but couldn't and felt that warm sensation
again. He realized that the plaster of mud and blood
caked over his thigh was all that had saved him from
bleeding to death. The croc had disappeared - but not for
long.

He was not yet rotten enough to eat! He struggled to open his eyes into the darkness around him. Through the narrow top of the shaft he could see the stars. He must escape or be eaten, perhaps tomorrow or the following day, depending on what else the crocodile could find to satisfy its hunger in the meantime. He shouted and shouted and heard nothing but a feeble voice that came back to him and sounded like his own but didn't seem to be connected to him. Kunaynee wept with weakness and fainted again.

A scruffy, small dog snooped along the river's edge in the early morning searching for some extra scraps of dead fish for his breakfast. He was always hungry. He was fed on grains, if at all, and except for feast days got no meat and even then it was a tossed bone of a goat or a sheep and well picked over. But he never forgot the scent of meat and did a lot of hunting on his own as African dogs are expected to find their own food if they wished to survive.

His keen nose soon sensed the odor of fresh blood. He followed the scent to the higher banks of the river and discovered a small opening partially overgrown with tough green cactus. He crawled cautiously through the sharp outcrops of granite and dry cactus thorns. The earth was friable and his front paws dislodged pebbles and lumps of dried soil. Retreating in panic before he fell into the hole and tearing his fur on the thorns, he nevertheless still smelled raw flesh in the depths of the cave. Like all dogs who find something they cannot handle, he barked and barked well into the morning till he was exhausted.

He lay crouched near the top of the shaft till he saw shepherds pass and then began barking again but they did not hear him and passed on. Late in the afternoon, shepherds of Kunaynee's village were scouring the banks of the river. He had been missed and they were thinking mainly of hyenas who will attack a body that has fallen into a ravine. They were not thinking of crocodiles because shepherds knew all about them having to take their cattle to the river every morning of their young lives.

The little dog barked and howled beside the cactus and eventually alerted the shepherds who suddenly came over and peered into the dark shaft but could see nothing below except a pool of stagnant water. And all the while the dog kept pawing and sending showers of pebbles and dried earth down into the dark hole. The boys decided they must go down. So tying their grass whips together they made a long rope. One lowered himself halfway down into the shaft and saw what looked like a body below. Was it Kunaynee? It didn't move and didn't seem alive. He yelled for another to go fetch a basket and for two more to come down as well. With three of them dangling in the shaft they waited while a boy ran to the village and returned with a large, shallow grain basket which he threw down the shaft. The three, standing in the muck of mud and blood, placed the limp body in the basket and securing it with grass ropes waited while the ones on top raised it out of the cave and then climbed to the surface themselves. But of all this, Kunaynee knew nothing.

He spent many months on a mat in the village and endured hours of silent pain which the little dog shared with him. The dog had followed them home and decided to stay. It sat with Kunaynee all day, slept with him during the night and shared his bowl of food. When he could walk again, he walked with a cane, dragging the remains of his leg where the hip had been torn away by the crocodile.

'Well, Kunaynee,' said the stranger, rising slowly from the mat where he had left a good payment and picking up the basket, 'if you can outwit a crocodile you can do just about anything else you want. Remember my other baskets. I'll be back.' And he was.

By the time Kunaynee was twelve, he owned a little shop in the village. He sold only baskets and mats designed by himself. His designs were simple and vivid and never faded. Sometimes his basket told stories of the meadows and skies and sometimes only of the river where all life was. He called his shop Limpopo.

KORKORO BOY

Bashir was the most cheerful kid alive. He could never be unhappy for long, not even when he was slapped and he frequently was. He owned a wagon with four wheels made from empty beer cans that even rolled, complete with a plank on top and a somewhat deflated white football with black spots on it that some foreign lady had given him. He couldn't ride on the wagon. It wasn't strong enough for that but he could put small things on top of it and pull it around when he had time for playing and he had to stuff the football with dried grass and he felt rich. It wasn't every boy in the neighborhood who had a white football with black spots on it. And it was HIS football when they played together.

Bashir lived in a one-room hut in the market and he was quite content to have a roof over his head. The market was squalid and dirty, but he didn't care. It was the only place he had ever known.

He didn't go to school because there was none. So that took care of that. He had one outfit for clothes - a shirt and a pair of shorts, which his mother took off him occasionally to wash in the river and dry on the rocks which wasn't very often because he didn't have any other for this.

And he had a job which is a big deal when you're only eight. He was a korkoro boy and sent around to houses every day with an old string bag on his back and asking for empty cans and bottles. He would trudge along the streets shouting 'korkoro-allay' (anyone with any tin cans?) to announce his passing by.

His father always gave him a few coins in case he was charged for the tins. Many times the zabegnas and mameetas (guards and house maids) would ask for money knowing well that their employers tell them to give them away. But he was told to ask only. But in case - well he had a few coins to bargain for a good deal. His father specially wanted one liter and half-liter tins. Those were not always easy to find. He never cheated his father. It would be a rare day when he didn't give him back the coins.

His father had a shop in the market. He flattened the edges of the tins and sold them according to size to the women who needed them for measuring out what they sell - cereals and grains, oil, talla (home-brewed beer) and roasted pulses like peas, barley and suf. He also made household implements out of them that were specially sought after by folks from the countryside. He cut the large tins two- thirds down and fitted them with long handles to make small saucepans which women bought for roasting coffee as is the custom when friends drop by for chatting and just visit. The coffee beans were roasted over the hot household coals so all could enjoy the delicious aroma. They are then pounded in a small wooden mortar before being thrown into a jebena of boiling water.

Any bottles he could find were cleverly cut by a rotating string method and fashioned into drinking glasses, their edges being smoothed away with tuff, a volcanic rock found everywhere in Ethiopia. Even the tops were treated in the same manner and used for covers. His father was clever that way and made a simple living out of it, but it was Bashir who supplied him with his materials.

So he went out every day even in the rain and the cold of winter. At times he shivered a little but that didn't bother him. He was accustomed to the cold. He had no shoes but that didn't concern him either. No kid in the market had shoes and his bare brown feet were already so hardened and calloused, they could withstand anything.

Along with his happy smile Bashir was a little cheeky. He was cute and could get away with anything and used this to an advantage. He never whined or begged. Just asked for old tins. And with his appealing little face did a good business. Sometime the guards at big villas told him to go away as they wanted the tins for themselves or would make him pay a few cents so they could go out and get drunk. That was why he always shouted as loudly as he could 'korkoro-allay' so that maybe the ladies inside would hear. But mostly, he just accepted whatever the day gave him and was back in the market by sundown. One isn't to be in the streets of the market after dark.

He especially liked going to the foreigners'
residences. They always had many tin cans. All their food
seemed to come out of them. Perhaps they were too lazy to
go to the market with a basket to buy things and cook all day
like his mother did. Many of them didn't even save the cans
but threw them on piles of garbage over the walls of the big
stone houses. So he would search in those piles of garbage
and often find fascinating things he could keep and fashion
into playthings for himself. They threw out so much, those
rich people. That made any garbage pile an interesting place
for Bashir. He had only to take the tin cans to his father.
Whatever else he found he could keep for himself.

But there was something he longed to find and never
failed to ask and look for everywhere. A jerry can, either of
plastic or tin, to take home to his mother for her to fetch
water with from the river. The earthen pot she carried on her
back every day was so heavy, that already, she had become
somewhat bent and stooped. His father didn't even take note
of this because that was women's work. It was a plastic one
he really wanted because then his father couldn't take it and
flatten it into whatever he wanted to make. But finding jerry
cans was not easy, there were korkoro men as well as boys
and they usually managed to obtain them with some bargaining. Often, he would have to hide in the bushes when he
saw one coming else he would take his whole sack of cans
from him. But Bashir was good at hiding. Market boys were
smart at that and anyway he could outrun almost anybody.
So he continued to ask and hunt for his jerry can. Bashir was
stubborn and always had a determined expression on his
small face and what he wanted, he usually got in the end.

But today he wasn't interested in collecting cans.
Everywhere in the market they were preparing for Boohay.
The women had collected the special seasonal rushes from
the river or fields or from the little girls who came around
selling them for the Boohay bonfires as is the custom. They
were also baking spiced bread which they wrapped in the
leaves of false banana and placed on top of three hot stones
over the coals of the open fire. It was the annual Boohay
celebration that takes place just two weeks before their new

year which is during the second week of September. This
celebration is especially for boys. With the tall stacked rushes alight the boys would all dance around them for good
luck in the harvest of the coming year and then they would
eat the spiced bread while sitting around the dying coals of
the fire.

Some of the boys who didn't live in the market
would go to the foreigner's district to chant and dance and,
if lucky, they would get a few coins or cakes after which the
head boy would ask a special blessing for the house and they
would all go home laden with whatever booty they had been
lucky enough to get. It sounded exciting and Bashir longed
to join them but he wasn't allowed. His father said it was
begging. Well, it wasn't begging. They chanted and danced
and asked for a blessing, so why was it begging? But his
father said no and that was that. Or was it?

The celebration of Boohay was supposed to be only
for young boys. But bigger boys and men were spoiling it by
going to the foreigners' residences and demanding money,
becoming quarrelsome and acting rowdy as they wanted
money for drinking and would chase away the small boys.
So the police had to forbid Boohay in those neighborhoods
because the foreigners were complaining that men were
causing drunken brawls. So often the small boys would be
chased away by the house guards and their chanting and
dancing would be for nothing or if they did get anything the
men would waylay and rob them on their way home.

Still the adventuresome persisted and especially if
they didn't have far to run to their own neighborhood. Bashir
was tired of Boohay in the market. He was eight years old
and longed for a little grown-up excitement.

Although a loner as one had to be in his profession,
he met plenty of boys on his long trudges throughout the
city. This morning someone had said to him:

'Come with us tonight. We're going to the foreigners'
houses. They give us lots. Generally to make us go away as
they're not much interested in our songs and dances and
usually slam the gates before we say a blessing on their

houses. We can run off if the police come. We'll wait for you in the bushes beside the gully at sundown.'

Bashir was excited and could hardly wait. He'd never been to the foreigners' houses at Boohay and anyway his father wouldn't allow him out after six unless there was some big celebration in the market. And his father wasn't pleased with him today. He had collected practically nothing as he was dreaming of the night to come. And his mother kept sending him on so many errands that he grew impatient.

It was already sundown and the meeting place was far off. So he told his mother a lie - just a little one - that he wanted to go with the market boys to help setting up the rushes for the Boohay bonfire. It was very late when he finally got away and hurried to the meeting place by the gully to join his companions. But there was nobody there. They must have gone.

Now Bashir felt very alone. More alone than he had ever been before. It was a misty night and the moon was barely showing. He should not be out that late at night and by himself. There were thieves and hyenas and the boys would already have been to all the houses anyway. But Bashir was never desolate for long. He would go by himself. But how could he make the noise of the dancing with only his own two small feet? It took a lot of feet and voices for that. However, having come so far he would try it alone.

He passed a few houses but at one they apparently didn't even hear him, and at another the night guard rudely told him to be off. They had had enough boys for that evening. There was only one other house at the end of that street and he dared go no further. He had been there before collecting cans but he didn't know who lived inside.

So he cautiously crawled on top of the high stone wall and looked inside before venturing to the gate. It was such a splendid place! Did people live in such places all the time!

He guessed the boys had been there before because the people were building a fire of rushes and seemed to be having their own private Boohay. Did foreigners do that? The tall rushes were already alight and several young children and servants were gathered around. He didn't want to interrupt their private feast but it was his last chance. So he hastened to the big iron gate and began to chant and dance, but his voice sounded so thin and lonely and his feet weren't making enough noise to be heard.

A young boy answered the gate and shouted:

'Mum! There's just one small kid here. I'll let him in. I think it's the korkoro boy!'

Bashir timidly followed him in. He'd never before been inside a house with stone walls. It all seemed so grand. But nobody paid him any attention at all. It was already so dark and all he could see was the big bonfire of rushes and the scrambling of children like himself, only white. Or were they? Some looked a little brown, not as he was but not white either. They were all roasting buttered buns on the end of long sticks over the fire and those buttered buns looked so good and the fire so warm!

Some of the people sat on boxes, some on the grass or on the cement pavement and he himself was given some sort of thing to sit on which had an old cloth cover on top.

But he soon got up and edged closer to the fire. Then the lady, she must have been the lady of the house, took the old sweater off her son and put it around him and gave him a stick and he crowded around the fire watching how the others cooked theirs. Some were not very good at it and dropped them into the fire but quickly snatched them out and ate them, ashes and all. He himself barely cooked his, as he was so hungry. Then a servant showed him many little dishes of things he could put on his bun - meat, vegetables, spices and all sorts of strange food he'd never seen before. But he shook his head. A hot bun with butter was enough for him. It tasted like cake. He ate half of it and then put the rest in his pocket as he thought that was surely the end of the party and he should go. But no! He was pulled on his feet from beside the fire as the rushes were being burnt down and everyone had to dance around the blaze. That, Bashir could do better than anyone. And when they were finished he shouted out his blessings on this kind household and turned to go. But the feast was not yet over.

Someone shoved some fire sticks into his hands. They put them in the coals for a second and then sent them hurtling into the darkness. Bashir loved that and could hurl them further than anyone else. The servant brought out some hot cake and all the children were given a drink from cans which they tossed carelessly aside when they'd finished. Bashir eyed those cans being just thrown away anywhere and hoped the lady would save them for him tomorrow but he didn't ask. He was so bewildered with the whole party he only clutched his cake and forgot to even finish his orange drink sitting by his feet.

It was only then he nervously and curiously fingered the old cloth beneath him and lifted the edge and found to his amazement that he was sitting on a jerry can and a new one too! And it was a plastic jerry can and it even had a lid. Surely they didn't need it? They must have many grand chairs to sit on inside that house. And he suddenly felt such a mixture of excitement and terror - excitement because there was a jerry can right under him and terror because he mightn't get it. He didn't even notice that for some moment the lady was telling the tired and cranky children, too overloaded with merriment, that it was late and time to go home and the guards from their own houses had gathered and were waiting at the gate to take them there. Although Bashir himself was also full of food, fun and flares, he couldn't take his eyes off that jerry can and fondled its smooth sides totally lost in such good luck. The blessings he had asked on this kind family seemed to have fallen on him.

He considered it all the time as the children were being hustled out the gate.

He thought: "I wish I could buy it, but how much would it cost?"

Bashir didn't deal with anything more than pennies. And with his small head twirling with such possibilities he was suddenly aware of the guard nudging his shoulder and telling him it was time for him to leave also. He stood up, took off the sweater and bowing, handed it to the lady.

'O No!' she protested, ' you can keep it.'

Bashir felt grand and cozy in that long sweater which was long enough to cover the bottom of his shorts. But there was that jerry can. Should he ask? How could he? He had been a guest and had been treated like one and she had already given him the sweater. He fidgeted till the other children had gone away with their servants. The lady seemed busy and the guard again was trying to hustle him out and onto the road.

His hands were nervously clutching into fists inside his pockets and there he found the coins his father had given him for the day. He had forgotten to return them in his hurry to be off. He would offer to buy it! He seized the coins as if they would disappear through the threadbare pocket and held them out in his sticky hand to the Madame and with his daring, disarming smile pointed to the jerry can.

'O No!' she replied again 'I gave you the sweater. You don't have to pay for it and now you must go home. It's late for a small boy to be out.' She hadn't understood.

'But Madame, could I buy that jerry can? I have twenty-five cents.'

'You must go home. It's dark and dangerous for you to be out.' She still didn't understand. Which was no wonder. What would grand people like that do with an empty jerry can? It wouldn't be important to them and only for throwing away.

Bashir was determined and dug his small hard toe into a crack in the pavement. He didn't get a chance like this every day.

'But I want to buy it now. I must buy it now. I want to give it to my mother,' eying the guard who was hovering nearby and whom he guessed wanted it for himself, 'Madame, I have twenty-five cents,' he pleaded.

There was a brown man who seemed to be supervising everything and was listening. He must be the head servant as he was ordering everyone else around and seemed kinder than the guard. When Bashir told him why he wanted the can, he said that he was a very thoughtful boy and of course he could have it but must come and get it in the morning as some one could take it from him on the way home.

'No Sir,' Bashir insisted. He had seen such cans before at the gates of big houses and knew that the guards sat on them during the day. He would never get it in the morning unless the lady was around. And he knew - such a grand lady might be sleeping then. And like all kids NOW was this minute for Bashir.

'I..I just live five minutes up the street,' he lied smoothly. He would never have been allowed to take it if they knew he lived some two miles away in the market. He was a little scared but didn't show it. It was late and spooky to be out alone, but he knew many secret paths and, being a poor boy, no big thieves would bother him. And with his belly full of fun and food and opportunity Bashir felt more daring than usual and he wasn't going to leave without that jerry can now that it had been promised to him. And anyway, what was he going to tell his father?

'You live in our district?' asked the brown man, 'I haven't seen you before.'

Bashir nodded. Well he didn't say it. That was only two lies, well two and a half, he had told that day.

'O! Well in that case you may take it now but we'll tie it on you so it will be easier to carry on your back.' And they secured it on his back with strings across his chest and then bowing again with some difficulty, he hastened through the gate where the scowling guard was waiting to lock up. Bashir hastened up the hill.

He took no paths. It was too dark. He took the highway or what could be called a highway in the sprawling city. It was a paved road that had a few lights but the

distance between them was long and dim and the lights
themselves seemed to shift and it was a misty, foggy night.
There was a moon but it was overshadowed and only came
out occasionally for a passing moment.

He made a quaint little figure struggling along under
those blurred street lights that he knew could go out
anytime. That often happened in this city. That didn't bother
him much in the market, although it made some places more
dangerous. In his parents' one-room shack they used candles
anyway, but at this moment he hoped those streetlights
wouldn't go out. He trudged along the road, scooting it fast
between the lights. But he was somewhat overburdened with
the can on his back which seemed to get heavier all the time.
He was so small and the can outlined his shadow till they
became one hunchbacked shadow. Now his cheeky bravado
had faded and he was more than a little scared. There were
big hyenas that crept into the city at night to prowl and quar-
rel over the garbage piles and at that moment, he himself was
not much else. There were thieves also but what would they
want of him?

He paused under an eerie street lamp that flickered
weird shifting shadows around him. He had to have a rest
and do a little thinking. What was he going to tell his father?
Well, he still had the twenty-five cents and he had the jerry
can for his mother and he had had a wonderful adventure.
Bashir couldn't be worried for long. He rolled over on his
side for just five minutes and was barely conscious of being
roughly rolled into the ditch by many hands belonging to
four or five men who must have suddenly come from the
ditch's other side or the bushes beyond.

'Hey! Little one! What have you got in that bundle?'
And they dragged him across the road and pushed him on
the edge, yanked the strings over his front and back till they
cut his skin, searched his pockets and took his twenty- five
cents and ran a hand across his throat to indicate they would
cut it if he said anything. He mutely nodded Ok, too terrified
to speak. They then threw him back on the road telling him
to be off and fast and they themselves disappeared into the
willows bordering the ditch. They were drunk and the ditch

was strewn with broken bottles. The men were shouting at each other while they ripped off the lid of his can and hastily put many small bags in it.

Bashir was dazed and bruised and cut and furious. They had taken his jerry can and his twenty-five cents! He scrambled to his feet and ran and ran along the highway and he was mad, mad, mad! He found himself weeping with fright and fury. He ran till he could run no more but had covered a lot of distance. He stopped, panting for wind while his eyes searched for some small path leading off to the market.

He wiped his dirty hands to get the tears out of his eyes. He wasn't scared anymore. But what an ending to his wonderful evening and his plans! He wasn't scared, but he was furious. Even a hiding from his father didn't concern him over much now. It was all over. He got up wearily to find his way home and was momentarily blinded by the lights of a jeep roaring up the road. It was a police van!

He dashed onto the road in front of it waving till it stopped.

'They took my jerry can,' he shouted,' they took my jerry can!'

'Out of the way, small mitmat!' shouted the driver, 'we're looking for bigger things than jerry cans.'

'But they have my new, white jerry can,' he protested and forgetting his promise not to squeal, added, 'and they're there in those bushes beside the ditch!'

'O really?' they were suddenly interested. Small boys are good informers. 'Then run off home, brat! Or we'll load you in the van also!' And they roared off in the direction he had indicated.

Another boy would have fled wherever. But not Bashir. He wanted his jerry can and there might be more adventure to the evening if it meant he could get it. He crouched in the ditch and watched.

They stopped at the willows and there was searching and scrambling and even some shooting because one seemed to have escaped. The thieves apparently had something worthier than jerry cans but what could that be!

The police roughly hustled four men into the van along with several small bags they had dumped out of the can which they then threw aside. They were cursing because one had gotten away and there was more shooting. Bashir's eyes blinked and stared. They hadn't even bothered to take the can!

The moon suddenly came out full and clear and he could see it gleaming on the white upturned can. The van roared off and the moon went back to hide in the clouds and all was murky and silent again.

Dare he return to the ditch? Surely they had all been taken in the van. No, there was that one who seemed to have gotten away but he had been shot at and surely wouldn't come back. Bashir hoped he was dead. He crouched in the tall grass and thought and thought. He was certain there had been five men and saw only four being loaded. He waited and watched a long time in the deserted dark of the road and avoiding the highway crept back along the ditch.

It was all quiet and empty except for broken bits of bottles cluttered every where in a scattered debris and there, shining white in the lamplight and carelessly tossed in the ditch grass was his jerry can and a little further off near the road, the lid. What could the police have been searching for that is more precious than a jerry can, he wondered. But he realized why the thieves wanted it. Who would search a man with a jerry can on his head? He carefully picked his way through the broken glass to seize it, but suddenly a snarling shadow over towered him.

The one that had gotten away had returned to his rubble. He was bleeding and quite drunk, so drunk that Bashir dived expertly through his staggering legs and sent him face down into the remains for the broken glass and himself landed on all fours behind him cutting his own hand while getting onto his feet. Then grabbing the can and the lid, and deciding that the highway was no place for him ran a short way along it and chancing a small path through the bushes hoped it would take him to the market. It did and he arrived at the small door of his home and knocked a little fearfully. His father opened the door and cuffed him heavily.

'Where have you been?' he asked angrily.

But Bashir, being Bashir just staggered in with the can and dodging his blows said to his mother:

'I've been out...looking....well looking for a jerry can.'

'And where do you find a jerry can at midnight?' shouted his father while his mother shielded him from more clouts.

'In a ditch, father,' he murmured, still breathless.

'And that sweater? I suppose you found that in a ditch also?'

'You'd be surprised, my father, what there is to be found in a ditch.'

And Bashir, having rolled over onto his mat was asleep.

Next morning very early, even before his mother had gotten up to go to the river, and without his breakfast, he sneaked off on his route. It would give his father time to cool down especially if he could get all those tins from the party. And there was that twenty-five cents to explain. He'd have to think about that one. In his fury, the night before, his father had forgotten all about it. Should he say he'd had to pay for the jerry can? No, he'd told enough lies already. Why O why did it have to be on the night of Boohay he'd been robbed! His father would really think he'd been on a spree, which, he admitted to himself, he really had been.

He set out immediately for the lady's house and hoped she would be up. He was lucky. She was working in the garden and opened the gate herself.

'Why Bashir! You here and so early! I've collected all the tins for you in a pile here by the gate. Bashir! What happened to your face? It's all scratched! Did you fall last night on your way home?'

'No..oo, Madame. I was fallen,' he replied somewhat lamely.

'No, Bashir. In English we say 'I fell'. But come in and let me clean up your face with some medicine.'

Bashir considered his own explanation more accurate but followed her in and said nothing further while she swabbed his cuts and scratches with something that stung and examined another on his hand.

'This one needs a band aid. Almaz! Bring me the band aids...And O yes! The rest of the cake and the buns we didn't eat last night.'

'The bandaids are finished, Madame.' Bashir hoped the cake wasn't.

'Then go to the souk. No. Bashir can go himself. Just bring me twenty-five cents from the household change in the kitchen.' The servant returned with the money and pieces of cake and some buns.

'Now Bashir, I've cleaned your hand and put on good medicine. But it needs a band aid. On your way up, stop at that little souk and buy a few band aids and ask the souk man to put one on for you. I've put on a small bandage for now. And do be careful!'

Bashir loaded all the tins in the sack on his back and with two bags of cake in his hands and twenty-five cents in his pocket, climbed slowly up the hill and past the souk where he didn't even stop. He would soak his cut hand in the river where he could play all day since with his sack and his belly already full, he hadn't a thing to do till he went home early at nightfall.

THE WAY TO THE WELLS

Ramallah was beautiful. Large, searching black eyes set like gems in her classic face, long thick braids reaching below her waist, slim hands with hennaed palms somewhat roughened by daily heavy chores and a slender, graceful body that looked almost fragile, but wasn't. She was as pure as a figure often found on scraps of Grecian pottery unearthed in the ruins of old Jericho.

But Ramallah didn't know she was beautiful. Nobody had told her and she certainly didn't have a mirror to gaze at herself. There was little time for that anyway in the Palestinian refugee camps where she had lived all her eleven years. She had never known her parents. They had been killed in a border raid shortly after she was born and she had been taken in by some woman who ran a guest hostel on the edge of the camps where Ramallah had worked as a servant for as long as she could remember. The woman was kind enough and anyway, Ramallah's life couldn't be worse than that of the children around her. They were all poor and lived in the never-ending huddle and squalor of gunfire and bombs. It all seemed to go on forever and the children understood little about it.

Actually, she lived a better life than many other children in the camps. She had a more permanent place to live although she worked for her food and shelter and the work was harsh as it was for all Arab women. There was little affection and no caresses but growing up without them, she didn't miss them as she'd never known that kind of life. There was however a silent bond of loyalty in the guest-house which they all felt but never talked about. It was also understood that there were no gifts of money or anything else except for the owner - on which she fed them all. There were a few other children there too, but not many and they all had no time for playing. Not many guests passed by the camps as there were a couple of small hotels in the town and most stayed there after sweeping through the camps taking notes and pictures of their nomad misery. But occasionally, there were some who spent a few nights at the guesthouse so they could get to know the people and their condition better.

She was walking along the broad, flat, straight and long road to the wells just outside old Jericho, her tall pitcher balanced gracefully on her lovely head and clad in a pale blue homespun gown which modestly reached her ankles, and her head covered in a white cotton shawl both for the heat and also in case she should encounter any men on the way and could cover her face. Her ankles and fingers and ears were not adorned with any jewels or bangles although like any maiden, she longed for them. But where was she to find such finery? Only the soles of her feet and the palms of her hands were hennaed. It was early morning and the mountains on either side of the road left still a shade in the dry ditches where towered the occasional dark green palms.

It was such a perfect setting but she didn't need one. She walked swiftly in her bare feet and with a dignified litheness which was all wasted in that desolate place. Well, it wasn't wasted really because it was her background and beauty cannot be wasted. It gives an unconscious completeness where there is little else. And Ramallah didn't know that while walking the way to the wells, she was creating a painting that would endure forever on the canvas of someone's memory.

She scanned the long road ahead to spot the exact turning to the wells. There were a few camels on the road today and she always sighted the by-pass because they usually ambled there to supply themselves and their drivers with water. It was still far off and so she walked with an even measured pace as she had many trips to make that day.

Then she saw in the distance, a figure sitting in the shade of one of the shorter spreading palms. It wore a white kaffia and only men wore kaffias. She quickly drew the edge of her shawl over her face leaving only her eyes visible and prepared to hurry past.

'Salaam!' greeted a soft voice which was clearly not that of a man. It must be a tourist as they quickly adopted the kaffia to shield them from the sun. Strangers seemed to wear what they pleased.

She allowed herself a glance aside and saw a lady - or was it a lady? She was dressed in rough white trousers and sandals which did not come from Jericho. She had long golden hair, half concealed under the spreading kaffia and her face was very white. Despite her rough clothing, Ramallah noticed a large ruby on her pale finger and gold on her ears and snuggled inside her open shirt was a pendant of black Erzurum stone. She was eating a bar of chocolate and offered half of it to Ramallah. Although she had been told never to take anything from a stranger and was a bit scared and shy, Ramallah accepted it as it was long yet till eating time when she would dip flat bread into mutton stew. And she longed for sweets.

'How far to the wells?' asked the lady in a broken Arabic half mixed with Turkish and gesturing to the water pitcher on Ramallah's head.

'Just there,' replied Ramallah, pointing to the way where a hard trodden path led off to the right.

'Then I shall walk with you,' and the lady jumped up and continued on the road with Ramallah.

Ramallah said nothing. Why should a foreign lady want to walk with her? Little did she know with her eleven years that the stranger wanted to walk with her just to gaze furtively on her lovely face. She had that black box which they all feared over her shoulder, but she didn't ask to point it at her. Sometimes they didn't ask and just pointed it anyway, but the polite ones asked permission. She didn't even ask her any questions except to ask her name and when Ramallah told her, she said that that was a graceful name and became her well. Ramallah pondered over that. Nobody had ever told her before that she had a pretty name. They continued in silence to the wells.

There the lady sat on the rocks beside the many gushing streams. She took off her kaffia and doused her pale face which was now turning pink and her long hair and cupping her hands, swallowed much water. She lay on the rocks amidst the confusion of complaining camels, quarrelling for place and the many brightly garbed women, maidens and children all filling jars of all size and chattering and departing. Her eyes saw much, but never did she take out her black box and her gaze never left Ramallah. She seemed to be fixing in her memory forever that lovely maiden filling her earthen jar with the waters of Jericho.

After Ramallah had bathed her face, her hair and neck and swathed them again with her shawl and mounted the tall jar on her head, delaying some time while chattering and laughing with the women, she turned to go. The lady got up to join her.

'I'll walk back with you to the town. You wouldn't want me to get lost in your country, would you?' she smiled as she remarked this in her strange Arabic. And they started out on the way back to the old town.

The lady was obviously tired but ashamed to show it. Ramallah slackened her pace a little and pointing to her jug, asked if she wanted some water but she refused. She found another bar of chocolate in her pocket and shared it with Ramallah and they both laughed because it was by now melting, and their fingers were sticky so they wiped them on the grass by the wayside. When they came to the first shack on the outskirts of the town with its rough signs of lukewarm Coca Cola, the lady said goodbye but first asked Ramallah if she would like a bottle of coke or an orange drink or whatever they sold.

She shook her head and the exhausted lady said goodbye again and Ramallah continued on her way. She had been away long enough and couldn't be caught drinking bottled drinks by the wayside and with a stranger. But O! How she wanted to! And she wondered about it all as she took a side road to the camp. Who was that person? She thought to herself. Perhaps she had dreamed it all because Ramallah often took to dreaming on the way to the well.

'What took you so long?' demanded the woman of the hostel.

'It was so hot. I stayed overlong at the wells.'

'Well, tend to the toilet. We have many guests tonight.'

It was another of her tasks to see there was water enough in the jug by the washing basin and to empty the waste buckets. The bathroom contained nothing but a bucket with an old plastic seat, a wooden stand for a small jug of water and an enamel basin. There was an old rusty bathtub which didn't function at all but was too much of a chore to move and anyway there wouldn't be enough water to use it. It was a busy place in the morning if there were guests.

She disappeared quickly in preparation for the people to come. That night she heard a small crowd of them. Perhaps only three or five and then went to sleep on her mat.

By four in the morning, she sat there on the edge of the old stained bathtub braiding her lovely hair and the lady of yesterday pushed open the door. She stopped in astonishment. Ramallah didn't know what a picture she made, plaiting her long, dark hair in such surroundings. She left while the lady used the toilet and returned immediately to remove it. The sanitation in the camps was strict. But the lady seemed upset at anyone doing such a thing for her.

'You? Here?' she asked. Ramallah nodded.

'Tell me. Do you have a mother?' She shook her head.

'You are a servant?' She nodded a reply.

Then the lady searched in her handbag and put a handful of coins in Ramallah's hands. She shook her head again and handed them back. This was a guesthouse and except for food and a bed no one received gifts from the guests.

The lady removed a pretty scarf from around her neck and put it around Ramallah. Silently, she returned it. She offered her a small bar of soap which she knew was scarce in the camp and a bottle of perfume from her bag. These were also refused.

'Don't you wish to remember me?' the lady pleaded.

'Yes,' replied Ramallah, 'I do.'

Someone else was already banging on the door of the only washroom.

The lady poured a little, but very little water in the basin, remembering well the child who carried it and who must dispose of it. Then removing her ring, she hastily washed her face and hands and departed.

Others came and went and soon Ramallah was left alone to clean the washroom. She wondered sadly if she would ever see that lady again. She could hear them talking in the outer room and heard them saying that they were going to the wells and then on to old ruins beyond. They wanted to photograph them at sunrise and they would not be back as they would go on from there. So settling their accounts and saying goodbye to the owner and in a whirlwind of luggage, they left for a waiting, dilapidated dolmus outside.

Ramallah returned to the washroom and lifted the basin to dump out the dirty water and clean it and her eyes widened in dismay. There beside it, was the lady's ruby ring. The early morning shadows of the washbasin had concealed it and in her haste she had forgotten it.

What was she going to do with it? She turned it over in her hands and how it glowed red in an escaping ray of the not yet risen sun! For just one moment she slipped it on her finger, just to feel what it felt like, and it nestled so naturally on her bronze skin. Then she hastily removed it. Should she give it to the hostel woman? No! She would return it herself. She dashed into the outer room and demanded:

'May I go for the water now?'

'Why so early?'

'It's going to be hot and you know with so many guests, they've used up all the water.'

'It's not even sunrise. You'll become lost.'

Lost on the way to the wells? She knew it well. Hadn't she begun when five with a smaller jug?

'Are you just wanting to go for a walk? Have you finished cleaning the washroom?'

'Yes.' Well, she hadn't really.

Permission was slowly given for the woman was reluctant to allow a young girl out before full daylight. However, she consented for she trusted Ramallah.

Breathless, she draped her white shawl over her head and shoulders and was out of the door where she found her jug and perching it on her head went slowly on the path. Once out of sight of the house, she put the jug under her arm and ran and ran till she came to the long straight road that led to the wells. Fortunately there were many camel trains slowing the traffic that morning but dolmus after dolmus swept past her and dodged the camels ahead. They wouldn't stop if they were full and they wouldn't stop anyway for a woman water carrier as she would have no money. She let her jug roll into the ditch and sat by the roadside under the palm tree of yesterday and waited.

Maybe they had stopped to buy some supplies? No. it was too early. Maybe the lady had remembered and returned to the hostel and what would she think if the ring was not there? She should have given it to the hostel woman else they all would think she tried to steal it. And that would be a disgrace to an Arab house. O why hadn't she stopped to think of that!

Another dolmus passed her but paused a little way down the road. She ran after it, forgetting her jug rolled in the ditch. Was it the camel train that had stopped it? But no! It was backing up.

It stopped and the lady leaned out of the window.

'Why Ramallah! What are you doing on the road so early?'

Ramallah thrust her hand through the open window and gasped, 'Your ring, Madame! You left it beside the wash basin this morning.'

The lady had not even remembered she had forgotten it in the scramble to get away before sunrise. She took the ring and laughed at her own carelessness. Then she got out and putting her arms around the young girl hugged her closely and kissed her soft cheek and then got back into the dusty cluttering dolmus.

Ramallah watched it roar away with the lady still waving from the back seat while the dolmus swept and curved around the camels who were in no mood for leaving the side grass and were now sprawling over the road and then it continued out of sight:

She had put her hand to her check to keep the warmth forever and for long after she remembered that little palm tree. She often paused to rest there. Did she think the lady would be back? No, she knew she wouldn't. The memory was enough.

THE END OF THE STORY

Olana pushed his bony, complaining cows off the highway and into the muddy ditch. They should not have been grazing there at all and could have been forgiven for wanting to try the other side. His father told him every morning to keep them far away from the road. But Olana did not heed him much because he wanted to watch the cars and trucks passing by. There were not many, only an occasional one and sometimes not even that during a whole day.

But today was Sunday and those pale people from the city would be coming to sit on the grass and eat in the countryside. They ate fascinating things out of colored boxes and sometimes there were leftovers - a chicken bone, a half- eaten piece of bread that always tasted like cake to him and anyway there were always the boxes. He just hoped they would have something extra to throw away. Why they wanted to eat sitting on the grass he could not understand since he had heard that they had such grand houses to eat in. Anyway, even if they swept past without stopping and did not throw anything, it was more interesting trailing his three cows beside the big road than away from it in the meadows and the hills where he could see nothing. O perhaps he could have heard the voice of God like the shepherd prophets the priest told him about, but Olana was more interested in the voice of the far-off city.

Someone was certain to be passing by. If not cars, then there would be people returning from the market, their tired, patient donkeys trotting wearily but happily, having left their heavy burdens in the market behind and now exposing their chaffed backs to the sunlight while swiping a mouthful of grass from the roadside.And that offered a chance to talk to somebody and ask what they had seen in the big city.

They always had roasted grain in their pockets, which they shared with him while chatting. He cracked his jiraffe (whip) which he made by twisting river grass. It cut a sharp noise in the thin highland air. But his cows were so accustomed to the sound they paid no attention. So Olana lay by the ditch and waited. He had all the time in the world. He was eight, as far as he knew, had never been to school and would probably never have that chance and this was his one and only game for the day.

He did go with his mother to the very small local village market once a week to help carry what she could find there which wasn't much. But it was nothing new for him anymore. His mother chatted for hours with other women while he had to wait in the shade of the one, tin-roofed shack. Herding the cows on the road was much more fun.

He flicked off the flies that had clustered on his face and chewing a thread of grass gazed at the dry, blue sky. It should have been raining but he was happy it wasn't. Rainy days were cold days for shepherds in the mountains. He had only a long shirt of rough cotton and his thorny cracked feet were bare. He unhooked his precious safety pin from the cord around his neck and began to dig out the white eggs of the tropical bug that infests the heels of those who go barefoot in the country when suddenly his keen shepherd's ears heard a drumming noise that was not from the crowds of insects around him. There was something coming far down the road.

Was it a truck? Sometimes he hoped it was. The drivers tossed out orange peels and occasionally half or whole oranges but usually only the peels. He would dip them in the dark stagnant pools of the ditch and suck them all day. Sometimes a kindly driver would throw a handful of caramella (candy) but not always.

But this was not a truck. It was a people car and they usually threw out empty packages with pictures on them - pictures of strange children riding on wheels and sometimes of animals. He would save them and store them in some dry rocky place and look at them during the day. There was no light for looking in his father's round hut. Sometimes they threw half - empty bottles or cans and those he would finish and save for carrying water around from place to place while following his cows. But this car passed without throwing anything but clouds of dust.

He pushed a reluctant cow to the ditch across the way and didn't care whether it made it or not because he saw the sunlight being reflected on another car yet far away on the gravel road. He did see something thrown from the window as it went round the bend. It too swept past in a shatter of pebbles. Nevertheless it HAD thrown something and he hoped it was leftover, torn-up chicken bones. They never seemed to finish ‚ anything these foreign people. And it was past noon and his stomach dreamed of something special. He abandoned his cows and ran back to where he knew it must be.

He fished in the slimy reeds and dirty water till he saw it floating and caught up in the long grass. It seemed brightly colored, but it was not a box. He squelched through the mud to get it. It was something he had never really seen before. It was a book - a slim, tattered and torn book, already soaked in ditch water. Still standing in the stagnant water, he shook it and smoothed it carefully. Then remembering his cows, he hastily concealed it under his shirt and hastened back up the road. The people might have made a mistake and come back to get it.

He sat there by the side of the road, turning over the sodden pages and studying them with amazement. He had never really seen such a pretty book. In fact, he had never seen any at all except those old books with stiff yellow pages and wooden covers that the priests carried and no one could read but themselves. But this one had bright pictures. Why did they throw it away? Perhaps they could get another tomorrow. He carefully placed it on a warm rock in the sun to dry but couldn't wait till it did.

The pictures were of strange people. Very strange people. Their clothes were so bright and clean and different and they themselves pale like those rich ones driving past. As he turned the pages, he guessed there was a story in their strange language. Although he couldn't read his own language he knew by looking that it was not the same. It must be the ferenji's (foreigners') language. He had seen it on the sides of trucks passing by and just assumed they all spoke the same way.

What were all those grand ladies and men doing in that big stone house? No, it was a castle. There was one in the market. Kings had lived in it long ago. But it was old and empty now. This one was new and shiny and full of people but what were they doing? Didn't the men have to plough with the oxen in the fields and the women pound grain with big wooden pestles?

They must have many servants to do the work for them, he decided. Perhaps they were kings and queens. Yes, one of them certainly must be since he had a crown on his head and everyone was bowing in front of him. Olana had never seen the king but there was a picture of him in the local market. But this one was so young and wore an embroidered robe like the priests on feast days. Must have many cows, that one. And it WAS a feast day because all around them were tables of delicious food - chicken, meat, cakes and whole oranges with their insides in them. And off on the edge of all the pictures were little shepherds playing reed pipes like he often did himself but where were their cows? Even the shepherds were well dressed and wore little pointed caps and red shoes with turned - up toes. They looked so chubby and rosy and happy.

He turned back to the first page. It was half ripped away but there was a young very pretty girl with golden hair and in a ragged dress and bare feet like his own, sitting beside the coals of fire on the floor, just like in his own hut and there were dirty pots all around her. Did white people have to wash dirty pots? She looked very sad. In fact, she was crying.

Mean-looking, ugly women with good clothes were scolding and pointing and laughing at her. On another page there was a small dark, ugly creature with a hooked nose and black robes and it was talking to her. It had a pointed stick in its hand. Ah, Yes! That must be the witch doctor. Like all shepherds Olana, had a lively imagination and it had already begun to form a story.

On the next page, there was another picture where the witch doctor took her stick and waved it over a pumpkin near the wall and turned it into a house on wheels; then she waved the stick over some mice who were running around in the corners and turned them into four white horses. Yes, witch doctors could do things like that if you gave them enough money. Olana was becoming excited and could hardly wait to turn the next page. Then the witch doctor pointed her stick at the pretty girl in rags and she had a beautiful white dress and white shiny slippers and was riding in the house on wheels. The following page showed her at the feast and the king was bowing to her. But on the next, someone must have beaten her for she was frightened and running away and the handsome king was chasing her with one of her own shoes.

Why was she running away? Didn't she like him? Olana was roughly roused by a truck driver shouting at him because his cows were on the road again. 'It's you who needs a shepherd, you ass!' he yelled at him while passing. Olana had forgotten all about them. He chased them off with a few stones and returned to his treasure.

The pretty girl was beside the coals again and wearing her ragged dress and bare feet and all the black pots were around her but she was not washing them. She was looking at one slipper in her hand and probably wondering where she had dropped the other. And the pumpkin was the pumpkin again and the mice were running all over the place looking for grains.

She had been having such a good time at the feast, until she got frightened and ran away and lost her slipper. And it was the witch doctor's fault that she was crying beside the coals. They shouldn't start something they can't finish properly. She had given her a lovely dress and it turned back to rags and those mean, ugly women would make her wash the pots again.

It was Olana's opinion that the witch doctor wasn't very reliable. She probably wanted money. They often did that. They half - finished a job and then asked for more money to finish it. And the pretty girl didn't seem to have any money. However, he had to see what happened so he turned another page. There was the king looking very angry indeed and watching the mean ladies and others throw their shoes in a pile. They were trying on the white slipper that the king must have brought with him. They were all pushing each other and trying to snatch the slipper. But their feet seemed to be all too big.

Despite his fascination and curiosity, Olana's eyes were drooping. It was now hot and he had been out with his cows since early morning. He dozed off on the coarse grass of the ditch with the book still on his chest and dreamed of grand ladies with many shoes and all in a pile and the king searching in the pile for the white slipper while he, himself, was trying to help the king.

A rustle of evening wind blew over a curled and now dried page and he was startled awake. It had become dark and he looked around in dismay. There was no pile of shoes. Only his cows huddled forlornly in the ditch. Was his book a dream also? No, it was there, fallen by his side. He seized it to make true his dream and find out if the king had found the other slipper he was looking for. But the remaining pages of the book had been torn out. He could find no more pictures and away in the hills, a lone hyena was howling. He shoved the book inside his shirt and hustled his cows out of the ditch and onto the path toward home.

They knew the way and needed no prodding so he took out the book to study the pictures again and see if he'd missed some pages. No, it was the same. But because of the last torn - out pages it had no ending.

He would have to think of one himself. He couldn't have his story ending with the king looking at a pile of shoes. Kings didn't do that. They would have a servant doing it for them if they had to wait longer than a minute.

He single filed his cows onto the path and thought awhile. He had it all figured out.

He would have the king demand back the slipper as the ugly women were spoiling it with their big feet. The pretty servant girl hides the other slipper in her raggy dress, picks up the pot and goes for water. The king notices her tiny feet and asks if she has seen a slipper like the one he holds in his hand. She takes out the other one hidden in her rags and gives it to him. For who can lie to the king? He insists she tries them on and, of course, they fit - they were the slippers the witch doctor had given her. It was all like a password in a spy story and Olana had heard plenty of those.

Then the king buys her another dress and marries her. There would be a big feast like the one he'd seen on the cover picture of the book and the shepherds would play their pipes and she, the pretty servant girl, becomes the queen.

But what about the slippers? They were the only things the witch doctor had allowed her to keep. And who knows with witch doctors? She might be back. Olana was uneasy about that part.

However, he wasn't having the witch doctor spoiling his story. She would come back and tell the pretty lady she could keep them till they wore out. But the pretty lady, now the queen, was smart. She put the slippers on a red velvet cushion and never, ever, wore them all her life. After all, there were carpets in the castle, not mud floors like in his own hut, so she didn't need them really.

A PLACE ON THE STREETS

He didn't really live anyplace. At nights, he loitered around the shabby Italian restaurant where the kindly owner sometimes handed out leftovers of splattered spaghetti scraps, stale rolls or an occasional meatball that someone had left uneaten.

She seemed to have remembered him from somewhere - a distressed boy with a despairing little face, half-stepping before her with some fumbled request then slipping back into the evening crowds because he was timid and she was indifferent.

Street boys were a pest. A casual glance, a little sympathy and they plagued her for evermore. There were just too many of them, wanting to guard her car or run an errand. They were full of information and could offer advice on anything. They always seemed to know what she had come to the city for and where to find it. If she wanted to see a certain person then they could tell her where to find him and they had a good idea about what time she would be leaving. They had to earn a living and this was the only way they could do it. But they were tiresome and too numerous even for the concerned heart.

She guessed the first time she had really noticed the little waif, was the night she left the restaurant. He was kneeling under the insect-coated street lamp, pulling from the pockets of his patched, baggy shorts his collections for the day. They were not many - a handful of clay marbles and a squashed bun. Hadn't she seen him somewhere before? It must have been months ago and there had been many other boys guarding her car since then.

He scarcely saw her and for this she was relieved. It was nearly midnight and no time for herself to be in that silent neighbourhood, let alone a small boy. But he was a vagrant who found his shelter in the alleys. She did not even pause but walked rapidly to her green Topolino and drove off and left him - a forlorn silhouette under the diminishing spread of a murky lamp in the deserted street.

Several nights later, she returned to the city to meet a friend. The boy was there, hugging his knees in the dark doorway of a closed shop not far from her habitual parking spot. The mountain night was bitter and there he could warm his bare feet on the wooden steps. Since she had to wait, she sat in the car and pretended to read with what scant light the streetlamps afforded.

That night, he had the street to himself. He left the doorway and ventured a few paces closer to her car. She knew he wanted to guard it for a few pennies but had to wait till she left it before he asked. Anyway, she had Gorky with her. Gorky was her dog. He always sat in the front seat and his job was to watch for the casual thief or to just keep her company and Gorky did not tolerate interference with his duties.

She gave Gorky a cookie which he didn't want but took in his mouth because to refuse it would be bad manners. He didn't know what to do with it so he dropped it on his rug to bury later. Outside, the small figure sauntered along the sidewalk, trying to pretend he was just passing by. His bare feet made no sound on the damp pavement; only his shadow told her he was there. From time to time, the occasional shafts of light from passing automobiles outlined him briefly.

He moved with the uncertainty of someone who had never had the right to be anywhere and who didn't matter much to anyone. Clouted by bullies and chased off by shop owners or the police, he probably put up with anything just to stay alive. He didn't seem to be aware of the poverty and squalor of his small world. In any case, it would probably be all he had ever known. But there was a patient persistence about him, clinging to a childish hope that had not yet been shattered. He so desperately needed a place on the streets.

He could have been about nine but had never really been a child. Yet he would have known a few boyhood treats. She had often seen these little beggars, warming their chilled feet on a charcoal brazier in the tiny Arab souks. For a penny or two, they could have a glass of steaming spiced tea and a piece of hot bread and a feeling of being rich like people who went into shops and bought fascinating foods which they carried out in large boxes. But he was too small to get many customers. It took a more sturdy lad to guard a car.

She wondered where he had found the new cotton jacket he was wearing. He seemed so proud of that jacket and kept fingering the shiny buttons on the breast pockets. She recognized it for cheap, smuggled goods bartered by hawkers from the bazaars. It would have cost forty cents perhaps - surely a sum he rarely had. It was too large for his thin shoulders and too long for the rest of him. But he had not rolled back the sleeves for they had brass buttons on the cuffs. With his shapeless shorts, scratched legs and rough bare feet, it was a strange outfit. He looked like a small scarecrow without the hat. She noticed that his head was shaven except for the tuft of hair that ran from his forehead to the back of his neck. Legend had it that St. Peter found it easier to pull these innocents into heaven that way.

The heat inside the car had begun to cloud the glass and Gorky put his head on her knee to inquire how much longer they had to wait. Alarmed, she realized how much time had passed and that they had better be leaving. She could no longer see the little urchin and concluded he must have wandered away. She started the motor and clearing the patch of fog on the side of the window, stared into two dark and curious eyes.

It was the curiosity of a child who can momentarily forget his misery when attracted by something new. He said nothing at all - just stared in wonder at their cozy comfort within. Perhaps he wondered what was inside or perhaps he thought that they might have something extra they didn't need. But he didn't ask and Gorky didn't snarl.

Searching in her provisions, she rolled down a window and handed him a bun. He bowed and cupping his hands accepted the gift in silence.

As she drove off she could see him in the rear view mirror, carefully buttoning the bun in the breast pocket of his jacket and watching her departure. Later, while driving home, she asked herself why she had not given him two or, for that matter, the whole bag.

Sometime later, she came late into the city and spent the night there. Early in the morning she came out to the street. She was impatient to get away. He was there, carefully wiping her car with a bundle of rags. She was annoyed and told him to be gone. She didn't need her car cleaned. He backed off, perplexed, a shivering little rag-a-muffin who had just wanted to earn a glass of tea for his breakfast and no doubt hoping that this had been his chance to be accepted by someone.

She drove off in a temper, furious at herself because she had had no change. Then why not have given him a dollar? Ridiculous! No one would give such a sum to a street boy. But she was not convinced. She could no longer get that boy out of her mind nor forget the white streaks of hunger in his small brown face.

He had huddled without sleep throughout the night. The covers he had made from cardboard cartons were not warm and he had had no supper. But he couldn't sleep because he was afraid. What was she going to say? Would he be turned away again?

At daybreak, he went to wash his head in the muddy, stagnant pool of the river where the women pounded their clothes to make them clean. He didn't wash everyday. The river was far from the shed where he found his shelter and there was always the search for something to eat in the morning.

But this was a special day. It was Wednesday. She always came to the city on Wednesdays. Surely she would remember him, he assured himself. Once long ago, he had guarded her car for two hours and she has given him many coins. He remembered the little dog sitting on the seat behind the wheel. He was not friendly, and so he had to stand a little way off. How proud he was, that little dog! But he was not a lion. He would have his throat cut if thieves came, while he could at least run away and return to tell her where they were hiding.

Why do the rich always look so clean he wondered as he smoothed the creases from his crumpled blue jacket with a handful of water. Perhaps they didn't have to sleep in their clothes? Or perhaps they lived closer to the rivers. She was always so fresh and lovely and had golden hair. Even the little dog's fur was so white and pretty.

He no longer thought much about being dirty, but did wish he had his toga to cover his grimy clothes so he wouldn't look like other street boys. She might not even remember him again.

He worried about this all the way to the restaurant and there he was not so lucky. He had been hoping for some leftovers - some cold spaghetti on a newspaper. But the friendly boss wasn't there. Only the cook and he was drunk and disagreeable.

'Be off! Beggar!' he shouted when he crept into the cluttered back entrance. 'There is nothing for you this morning!'

He walked away, shivering and humiliated, with his hands inside the long sleeves of his jacket. He didn't even have a name anymore. What was his name? He had begun to forget it. No one called him anything but 'beggar' since he had to leave his father's house.

He had never, ever been warm since the day he learned that his father's new wife had sold his toga and then told him to leave, so there would be enough room for her own children.

'But where am I to go?' he had asked her.

'Go!' she had screamed. 'Go make a living off the streets!'

'What can I do on the streets? Where am I to find my bread?'

'Beg! You are nine years old. Beg from the rich!'

'But I don't even have a toga,' he had said as he turned away.

He had been to school for one year and had learned his letters. But he didn't know how to beg and was timid and ashamed. He wanted to work but what could a boy of nine do on the streets where there were so many others?

They were fair enough, the street boys. But they had made fun of him because he knew how to read and they had never been to school. Nevertheless, they were much more cunning than he was. They knew how to whine and beg and how to make enough coins among themselves. They were a gang and they didn't want him but sometimes shared a little when he had nothing to eat.

He sat on the edge of the pavement in the hot sun but even then couldn't get warm. What was he going to say when she came? Should he beg and look miserable to make her pity him? The others did that. But she didn't like to be pestered by them. Anyway, it seemed like many Wednesdays since she had been to the city and so he had begun to search out other places where she could possibly have gone. And worrying about what he could say, he fell asleep by the curb and didn't even see her coming till she parked the little green car almost where he was lying.

Since it had been nearly three weeks till she could return to the city, she was out of provisions and parked by the new supermarket several miles from her usual stopping place. She locked the car and prepared to walk a few long blocks to the bank where she had to meet a friend.

But he had seen her, had seen her lock the car and quickly start off somewhere. He was so terrified he couldn't move till several other boys appeared from the twisting, hidden alleys just off the street and ran to surround her.

'O scram!' she shouted in an irritated voice and waved them away. But they didn't move far.

He HAD to do something. He scrambled to his feet and hurried till he was respectfully a few paces behind her. Nervously clutching a curl at the back of his neck he informed her in a timorous voice that the person she was looking for was not in the bank but in the bookshop opposite.

Exasperated but laughing she told him to go and guard her car. She started to explain where to find it but he had gone. He already knew where it was.

The other boys retreated. It was the law of the streets. No street boy would interfere in another's good fortune.

He leaned against the car which was hot from the sun and suddenly felt warm again. The little dog wasn't there. She never brought him when she remained in the city till morning. It would be a job for the whole night.

He watched her as she swiftly crossed the street among home-going crowds. Abruptly she stopped. He stood up in dismay. His throat dried out. Didn't she trust him after all?

But she only turned and gaily called back: 'What's your name? You!' she pointed to distinguish him from the other boys.

He hesitated, fumbling with a button on the pocket of his jacket, then shouted over the distance:

'They called me Daniel!'

MOONLIGHT ON THE WATER

They were not bright, not even of passing calibre and they had failed grade one again last year. They were dull and couldn't learn. The Dumas twins were now eight or nine years old. They guessed they were metis but didn't even know. The woman had shoved them out of the cabin this morning and told them to go to school.

'What are we going to do?' said Patrick to Peter, 'we have no pencils and no scribblers.' And certainly they had no lunch and felt ashamed. And empty because they had had no breakfast.

'Why do we have to go to school anyway?' replied Peter. 'We don't learn like other people. And it's now ten o'clock.'

'It's the law,' stated Patrick, not knowing what that was. 'The law says we have to go to school till we're fourteen. Then we can go fishing or trapping. But I'm scared this morning. There's a new teacher and they say she's very hard. And we're two weeks late. Nobody told us we had to go back to school again.'

They were a pathetic pair, the Dumas twins, climbing the now turning autumn hill that led to the school and arriving late. Not pathetic because of their ill-fitting, scattered bits of clothing, but their wan, gray Indian faces were too old for the small bodies beneath them. They knocked timorously on the open school door.

'Who are you?' demanded the teacher who seemed very severe indeed. 'Don't you know that school begins at nine o'clock?'

'We're Patrick and Peter and we've come to school.'

'Well, you are late. And where are your papers?'

'We don't...have any,' apologized Patrick. They had thrown them in the lake because they had failed again last year.

'You don't have any reports? How am I to know what grade you're in? Were you here last year?'

'They have been here for the last three years!' shouted someone. 'And they are always in grade one!'

'O silence!' warned the teacher, 'or you'll stand outside!' Well, not really, they had a roaring good time standing outside - 'or with your faces to the wall,' she added. But one boy had fainted when she had applied that punishment. With forty under-nourished students, she had forgotten all about him till he just keeled over. But now, turning to the two gaunt small faces she said:

'You may come in. You'll sit in the front desk before me and I'll put you in grade two.'

That required some moving and complaining as every pupil tried to sit in front of the teacher. They thought they'd get more attention and favors that way. But they were moved to the back nevertheless and Patrick and Peter were seated in front of her. She gave them a pencil each and a page of sums. Patrick could do sums but Peter couldn't so he copied and by recess they were done. She kept them in at recess and gave them a book apiece and they looked at each other fearfully.

They couldn't read and the pages were just a scattered mess of strange letters. Patrick handed back his book and really scared, stuttered, 'We cannoth read.'

When terrified, he had a lisp. Peter said nothing at all but had already closed his book and was rubbing off his dirty fingerprints from the cover.

Having many other pupils from grades one to eight, the teacher had no more time to spend on them. She handed them a piece of paper each to see what they would cover them with and passed on to the other classes. She cautiously glanced from time to see what they were doing.

Patrick had written PATRICK DUMAS on the top of the page and was carefully copying it neatly and in even lines till he reached the bottom. She turned over the page and wrote her own name on the top and told him to copy that. That took him till noon but he really worked on it and it turned out legible at the bottom. Peter, on the other hand, was busily absorbed in producing quite a remarkable pencil sketching of a cabin by the lake. He hadn't finished by noon as he was very careful about it, redoing some lines after smudging them out with his fingers being reluctant to wear out the eraser at the end of the pencil since it wasn't his. Actually his finger smudge added greatly to the picture he was making.

The teacher praised them both for their work of the morning and then closed the school for lunch. It was yet early autumn in the north and most pupils still went home for lunch except those whose parents were out on the trap line and these took their lunchboxes out and ate in the yard. She herself remained inside with her lunch but chased out all the children and closed the door so she could do some work. The twins respectfully returned the pencils which she put on her desk for the time being. Supplies were hard to come by in those days.

'What do we do now?' asked Peter of Patrick.

'I don't know. There's nothing to eat at home. But she's nice that teacher. She didn't even yell at us.' And they wandered off to the woods and ate fall berries still hanging from the occasional tree till they heard the bell ringing.

Peter worked on his drawing and was finished by four. Patrick was given another name to copy but was a little slower about it. He was so hungry and almost asleep. But Peter gave his drawing to the teacher and she held it up before the class saying loudly what a splendid artist he was and then pasted it on the wall.

This went on for another month and Patrick copied the names of every student in the class because they were familiar to him and was now copying sentences that related to life around him. Peter's sketches soon filled the walls of the one-room school. They often remained in the classroom during recess. The teacher allowed it as she suspected the others picked on them.

'Teacher,' remarked Peter one day while hanging around her desk at recess, 'Your hair shines like moonlight on the water.' It was such a spontaneous admiration!

'Why, thank you, Peter!' Peter didn't know why he was being thanked.

'Do you often watch the moonlight on the water?'

'O yes! On the long summer nights when it's round and yellow. It makes a golden path across the water! I sometimes want to run over it but Patrick won't let me. And then suddenly it's gone.'

'The moon goes behind the clouds and the path disappears,' agreed the teacher, remembering when she had had the same desire as a child and still did sometimes.

'The golden path goes behind the clouds,' reasoned Peter thoughtfully, 'because it belongs to the moon and he takes it with him. I guess it doesn't really get lost.'

The gusts of an early winter swept on them overnight and the woods were covered completely with heavy snow. There were no more berries left on the trees - even the clinging frozen ones had been taken by the squirrels and chipmunks and the other little woodland rodents preparing for the long winter. Old Papa Cann came every morning to the big stove and all the children brought lunch boxes and ate at their desks inside.

But the Dumas twins had no lunch boxes. They just hung around the stove and ate whatever was in their pockets or went for a lonely walk in the snow .

One day there was a terrible outcry at lunch.

'My mother gave me six sandwiches and there are only three left!'

'..and I had some chocolate cookies and they're gone!'

'..and yesterday I had three hardboiled eggs, my mother told me, and at noon there was only one!'

'My moose bone! We had moose meat for supper last night and she put in a bone for me!'

'It's the Dumas! The Dumas! The Dumas! Shouted everyone.

The teacher called the Dumas twins to her desk where her own lunch was already spread out.

'Did you steal from the other children's boxes at recess?' she asked, well suspecting they had.

'Yes.' It wasn't in their nature to lie about anything. Life was stark enough without being concealed by lies.

'Why?'

'Because we were hungry,' faltered Patrick, always the spokesman.

She did not give them a lecture on stealing. She gave them some of her own lunch instead, hoping it might induce some compassion but it didn't. They all hated the Dumas twins perhaps because the teacher favored them and had set an entirely new program for them since she really couldn't do anything else.

Everyone ate in silence, went out for a few brief moments and then classes commenced as usual. Well, not quite as usual.

'Teacher! You've forgotten our geography lesson.'

'O yes!' She recalled vaguely. She had been absorbed in her own thoughts all afternoon. Those boys couldn't endure any more humiliation - or starvation either. It was undermining their natural childhood responses to a life that was handed to them on a jug of homebrew. And she herself had very little money to spare for anyone.

She told them to wait after school to the glee of everyone. They suspected the Dumas would get a good thrashing. But they got none.

'Peter,' the teacher addressed the trembling twins, 'would you sell me your drawings for five cents apiece?'

'O yes!' glowed Peter, wondering what he would do with that almighty sum. He would be earning money and he wasn't even old enough to go fishing.

'But I won't give it to you,' continued the teacher, 'I'll buy you milk and bread for eating at school and occasionally - very occasionally, some jam and peanut butter.'

'Peanut butter!' exclaimed Patrick.

'And you, Patrick, will gather me small wood and twigs for my little house - five cents a bunch.' They knew the teacher lived in a small cabin with a pot-bellied stove and had to keep it roaring. 'But if you find me specially pretty wood, I'll decorate my house with them.'

And soon the teacher had scrapbooks of sketching, her walls were covered with handsome little wreaths of pine cones and frozen red berries and her pot-bellied stove was kept going with fallen wood from the forest and the twins had milk and bread with thinly spread peanut butter and jam and somehow they all got through the long winter.

Peter's pictures were now in color as the teacher had given him colored pencils ordered from a catalogue and like everyone else the twins had lunch every day at school and nobody knew from where it came.

And then came the break-up. It was a long break-up and foreshadowed a short summer. It was nearing June and they heard the people talking about the teacher going away.

'I hope she comes back,' wished Peter aloud.

'We must give her something,' declared Patrick, the practical,'but what? We have nothing. And she's leaving Sunday.'

And Peter, like always, thought aloud: 'She has enough of my sketches. I've done for her everything - her cabin, the school house, the lake, the village, the night lightening that dances in the sky, the fir trees...'

'The fir trees!' exclaimed Patrick. 'She loves little wreaths with the cone and the red berries that we gave her at Christmas. She kept them on her wall till they dried away. We'll make her two new ones - one from each of us.'

So they spent the whole Saturday afternoon in the forest, choosing, discarding, for everything was too large or too brittle, while a whispering baby pine watched them intently. It was now four years old and already spread out to a perfect conical shape.

'That's the little pine tree she likes. She always stops to gaze at it when she's walking in the woods. She wouldn't let us pull it out at Christmas because she said it was happier where it was. I think it wants to go with her.' And the little pine soughed softly.

'Well, she cannot take a tree. She doesn't have the place and what would she do with it? And it can't last forever if it's cut.'

But the little pine, with its spindle already emerging was pleading. It had gotten new spring needles, having dropped the dull green winter ones around it. The new ones were soft and a delicate green and so pliable. It inclined itself gracefully, caught in the path of a sudden passing breeze in the still, silent woods.

'Take mine! Take mine! Take mine!' it seemed to sough forever.

So they cut small branches and made two tiny wreaths and searched for baby cones beneath and sprinkled them with the eternal red berries which they secured with bits of wire. They were beautiful, soft and scented but would not last forever. But to two small Indian boys today was what really mattered.

It was late when they had finished and they hastened back to the cabin with the night already overhead. Each clutched his treasure while sleeping on a pile of skins in the corner. It didn't matter if there was little for supper. They were so excited with seeing the teacher's face as they stopped her while boarding the barge in the morning.

They woke to an uncertain sky and each seizing his wreath ran out of the cabin and down to the wharf.

There was no lake barge. Not anywhere in sight.

'Perhaps she isn't going!' breathed Peter hopefully.

'Where is the lake barge?' Patrick asked.

'Papa Cann decided to leave early. There's a squall brewing. It left two hours ago.

'And the teacher?' whispered Peter. Each felt a clutching in his belly. Squalls on the lake were dangerous and many drowned every year.

'O yes. She left too. Papa Cann got her out of bed hours ago. What do you guys want anyway?'

They did not reply but went silently back to the woods and hung the tiny wreaths on the proud little tree. It seemed to be waiting anxious and impatient and was already writhing in a sudden undercurrent of wind that should not have penetrated so deeply into the forest.

Overhead, the sky became dull and leaden - the color of a stranded trout that had lost its silver sparkle. The waves from the lake lashed the sullen rocks along the shore and sent their splashing spume sheeting inland and soon the whole village and forest were whipped in a white fury of sleet and the huge trees dropped their boughs heedlessly crashing in a scattered litter around them while enduring an hour of nature's uproar.

And just as suddenly it was over. The sun angrily slit a space in the clinging clouds and soon the lake was blue and covered with subdued white-topped waves. The only sound was a thousand riverlets of melting sleet rushing down to the water's edge.

The boys crept out from under the boughs where they had taken shelter. The two little wreaths still clung to the small, spunky pine tree, standing confidently upright throughout the storm and looking even more lovely streaked with the melting snow. Wordlessly they gazed at them blinking the sleet from their eyes.

They went slowly back to the waterfront, picking their way over frantic streams splashing the slopes while seeking their way to the lake. They said nothing because there really wasn't anything to say.

THE LAST RAINBOW

Khan played a merry game of pushing-off with the other boys on the riverboats. They could all swim of course. One didn't live beside the upper waters of the Brahmaputra and not know how to swim even when the waters were often icy especially in the spring. And more especially if you worked most of the day on the barges throughout the year. The other boys were kind enough most of the time but at other times, would tease him and call him the tongue-less one. For Khan couldn't talk. He could smile and he could hear but he couldn't talk and he couldn't laugh either. In all his ten years, he had never spoken a word. Nor had any sound whatever come out of his throat.

No one knew why and no one really cared. In a village it was like that. They just accepted what Allah thought fit to give them. Their disappointment was obvious on many an occasion and Khan knew early in his short life that he was a disaster to his family.

He was the only son in an already large family of six. His father had wanted him to become a merchant. He himself was a poor farmer working only for survival and a merchant was a class above that. But how could his only son become a merchant when he couldn't talk? Merchants have to bargain and be clever with their tongues and although Khan had one, it didn't seem to be of any use to him and because he couldn't talk like every one else, they considered him silly or stupid. Even the Imam who had daily classes in chanting the Koran for boys wouldn't even allow him to sit on the edge of the circle where all the boys gathered in early evening and sat cross-legged to recite. They were not taught to read - only to chant the Koran and count the abacus.

'Go away! Speechless one! Till Allah gives you a tongue!'

So he didn't try anymore for fear of being ridiculed away. He found some work instead. Most of the time he worked on the dock, cleaning barges that came up stream and loading them with fish to return and hauling out the sails and plaiting ropes. He liked working by the river. But often he was sent to the fields, which was women's work. He toiled silently beside them, planting and weeding the rice and harvesting it when it was ready for threshing and going to the hillside to gather firewood. But he preferred to fish off the docks and would sneak away to do that when he could.

He was strong and handsome and because of that was tolerated. But he often thought of the years ahead of him. He was already wise enough for that. Plans are made early in a village.

Two of his older sisters had already disappeared and although no one spoke about it, he knew they had been sold in some faraway place like Calcutta and where that was he didn't even know - nor what their fate would be. His other sisters were younger than he was but unless some rich men bought them, they would also be sold and there were few rich men near his village. It was not that his parents were cruel but there were too many children in the house to feed and every year there was another swinging in a grass bundle on the bough of a tree nearby where his mother worked all day in the rice paddy. And always they were girls. But what if Allah should send another boy and who could talk? Khan shuddered. Although he would still be the eldest son, he could not be given a piece of his father's land since he was not normal like everyone else. Perhaps he would be sold also to some men's house in the big city. No one spoke about those evil places but all the boys knew about them. And sometimes they would taunt him:

'You're getting big now and you're pretty to look at. Beware! One of these days you will be sent away. No girl will be promised to you. No one will ever build a marriage hut for you!'

These conversations would generally take place when the boys were sitting in circles plaiting bamboo for the walls of a new marriage house or just to replace huts that were so often washed away when the Brahmaputra went on a rampage in the spring. And often Khan would sneak away in tears and hide in the forest.

He felt somehow that this was not really his belonging place but being a village boy knew no other. So he would sit in the forest and carve birds and tigers and other animals he saw there and ponder about himself. Khan was an excellent carver but there was no one to buy his work. The merchants on the riverboats would sometimes buy it to sell downstream but they gave him so little. Merchants were like that. They cheated. He was lucky if he got one anna.

Khan loved the river. It was really his only friend and he would often sit there on the banks when the other boys were chanting their lessons in the evenings. The river was the life of their village. It was sacred to the Brahmins, but who they were he didn't know, and respected by the Muslims. Somehow it was HIS river. He loved it at low ebb before the monsoons and loved it with a certain fear when in full spate. But it was all the time HIS river and his only companion and where it went, he often wondered and longed to go also.

And from where it came he didn't know either. It was somehow just like himself. But it had a voice in fact, so many voices and Khan would sit there and listen to those many mysterious voices and think that someday he would find out where the river went.

He was sitting on the sheer embankment one early evening in the spring and counting the small islands that were disappearing, being swept away by the floods. But new ones would appear later when the waters subsided and he hoped they would be close enough for him to swim out to. The Brahmaputra was his friend and gave him new places to dream of and explore. But those islands, like his dreams, never lasted long.

It was by now grayish moonlight as Khan had forgotten to go home for supper and was dangling his legs over the sharp drop into the river. He was not aware of any danger. Didn't he sit there every evening? But the heavy thaws in the mountains had swollen the waters so that the treacherous currents under-cut the bank where he was perched. And suddenly, he was swept out clinging to a mass of heavy sod that was fast dissolving and out into the center of the torrent at least a kilometer across. He couldn't cry for help and who could help him anyway? He went down into darkness in the swirling water already laden with uprooted trees and dead animals and debris of inundated habitations.

Miles and moments later he was conscious of lying outstretched on the top of the disintegrating beams of a roof, its thatch long since torn away. He pushed his feet through the crossed rafters and clung, half-drowned to the surface beams and half dead with terror and cold and felt himself drifting swiftly with the merciless current.

It was morning when he realized he was still alive for a hot sun was splaying its beams over a narrow shore where the roof had crashed onto some boulders on a sharp curve jutting out on the river. Dazed and bewildered he disentangled himself from the sodden wreckage and gazed at an unusual place.

To him it was another country. It was a village but must have been miles and miles from his own and so different. There were the same rice paddies, the same bullocks standing around, and the same thatched houses but there were coconut palms and domed buildings with strange figures and symbols written on the walls and the roofs. This was Brahmin country. He had heard merchants from down river speak of the Hindus as they passed their villages along the way from the big Muslim country at the end of the river - if his river had an end. Khan always thought it went on forever.

But he had been beached on the strip of sand along with the smashed beams of the roof. He found a decayed banana that had drifted down a river-let and ate it. What was he to do? He was naked - his clothes and cap and belt dagger having been washed away and he couldn't speak. He was hungry. He would have to beg for some rice. So he fashioned himself a loincloth from the floating debris of the river and went slowly into the village to seek out the market. It was a much larger one than in his own village. There were not so many women sitting on the ground with their produce around them. Many had tables of bamboo and looked more rich than the women of his home.

But he was soon cuffed off when they saw he wasn't buying - only begging. They shouted at him in a curious language and became angry when he said nothing in reply.

This was no jungle village where a woman would always give you a bowl of curdled milk and a scrap of chappatti. In reality, it was empty of kindness for him. And since Khan was indeed empty, he ran off and sought elsewhere.

He ran till he stopped with fearful exhaustion beside one of those odd domed buildings with the bright writing on the top walls and curved roofs. What could be inside them? Khan, like all children, was curious but was by nature, timid. He looked carefully behind him. They were grand and beautiful but what was inside?

His belly told him it was no time to be timid. So he entered the building and drew back - horrified! There was a strange man, not looking at him, not moving, just staring over his head. He was some sort of a giant, three, four or five or ten times the size of Khan and not looking at him at all. Just staring at the opposite wall. And so since he could not speak to it he just stared back. But why should such a grand person speak at all to a naked river boy? He crouched in a corner and waited for him to turn and notice him but he didn't. He only continued to stare into the same wall beyond. He must be asleep, thought Khan, but his eyes were open. He wore red robes around his loins and over one shoulder and had necklaces around his neck and they hung down over his fat belly and he had four outstretched arms and hands, two were hanging with beads. On his head was something like a turban with a brilliant green jewel on his forehead. Carefully placed before him, were bowls of fresh rice and already wilting flowers. There were burners of live incense that scented and hung in the air like the mists on the river.

Khan went over and stood before him. He wanted to say: Master, could you give me some of your rice? But since he couldn't he put his fingers to his lips in a gesture of hunger and bowed before him. Still the man didn't move. So pleadingly, he put his head on its strangely carved feet, which were like the claws of a tiger and recoiled in terror!

The man was made of stone! Here was something like himself. He couldn't speak. But then he looked so mighty and important.

Dare he take a little rice from the bowls around him? Just a few grains. But then Khan couldn't stop. He emptied one bowl and then another and another. He didn't even feel guilty. The stone man wouldn't eat the food. And so he ate up all the rice sitting untouched before the stone giant even though he looked so fierce and angry in his red clothes. He didn't seem to care at all - just went on staring and didn't even look at him. Since he had many arms and hands, Khan guessed that if he couldn't eat the food with all that then he didn't want it.

Should he prostrate himself in thanks? But why bother? The stone man wasn't listening. Perhaps he didn't speak to naked river boys. Khan stepped back and gazed at him. He was a most peculiar person with those claws for feet. Khan himself could carve better than that. But the stone man continued to stare beyond all seeing and was not seeing Khan at all.

But he soon realized that someone else was. And they were not made of stone. Men appeared in the opening of that strange building. Men dressed in long, flowing trousers with bare chests on which hung beads and hair to their shoulders and long black beards. They were angry men and rushed and shouted at him and threw him out of what must have been their temple or their Mosque or holy place. And they cursed and screamed in voices that Khan couldn't understand.

Outside there was a sudden raining and he was pushed over the entrance and down onto a pile of refuse beside the temple. The refuse was made up of rotting, untouched fruit, wilted flowers and lumps of rice thrown in. They must be rich, he thought when he could think, to throw out all the food that the stone man didn't eat. And he wished he dared go through the whole pile and save some of it. But he had done enough already.

Stunned, he rolled over and landed on his bare feet. He paused only long enough to search for something that gleamed in the daylight and was not rotting vegetation. He dug down for it and found a knife with a broken blade. Even then he was risking a further beating because the red clad men were still pursuing him. He seemed to have spoiled their holy house but he wasn't certain. If he had been he would have prostrated himself and said he was sorry and hungry but Khan couldn't say anything. So being a practical jungle boy he grabbed the broken dagger and fled to the river.

There he hid himself in the jungle growth that held the riverbanks so close to the shore. With a full belly he lay concealed in the tangled lianas for hours. Suddenly he felt a strange movement in his throat. It made a sound and that sound was laughter. It must be laughter. He had heard it before among the boys on the boats when they were all playing and enjoying themselves. It must be laughter.

He lay there and marveled at himself. He could laugh! Therefore he must be happy. And he was. He had escaped and his belly was full of rice. And so he lay in the forest and laughed and laughed.

But Khan knew he had to leave and suddenly his laughter stopped. This was not a friendly village and apparently he had done something awful and could not be seen around it any longer. If he remained another day, Khan knew he would be recognized as the speechless boy who had been chased out of the market and whipped out of the holy house. And Khan knew what he had to do.

He fingered the broken knife still clutched in his hand. He had to go. But how? The cliffs were close to the river and so there were no paths except through the jungles above and there were tigers there and what was a small boy in front of a tiger who could even climb trees?

He went down to the river, his friend, the river. He tried again to laugh but couldn't. He didn't yet realize that there had to be some reason for laughter. The river was in a hurry and rushed past without speaking and he searched around with a kind of desperation for what must be done.

In all his short life, Khan had never stolen anything. At home he'd never even touched fruit or fish belonging to some one else unless being given permission to do so. But this was something else.

It was already dark and many dugouts were moored silently by the riverside and well up out of the current. With his half-knife, he slipped the woven mooring rope of the most sturdy one and with a pole nearby slipped it quietly into the river and stepping inside with nothing else, for he had nothing else, he joined the swirling current and headed downstream into the wild waters of the river.

He paused for a brief second and gazed at the sky. It was now late afternoon. The crowded clouds darkened the sky into an early night. The raining had stopped and there was a rainbow spanning the two sides of the canyon. A magnificent rainbow of many soft colors; a splendid rainbow to finish his harsh day and the beginning and the end of it were concealed in the towering forests above. He felt a restraint. Rainbows were sacred to his village beliefs and he ought to have paid it some reverence. But there was no time. Already the dugout was heading for swift midstream and he had to guide it to the safer shore where even there, the current was flowing back because of the under-force of the central stream. It was an hour before he got it safely in the backwater where with difficulty, he poled it forward enough to be carried downstream.

And then he looked again for the rainbow. It was gone and he felt sorrow and guilt in its passing. A rainbow was a sign of luck and of a safe passage to the other world but of which other world Khan was not certain. If it could only have waited a little longer for him. It is not every day there is a rainbow.

'River, my river,' he prayed silently, 'take me to your home' and he dozed at the bow but tried to keep awake in the cold darkness of the canyons.

He roused himself with a shudder because there was light. He thought it was morning till he saw the moon clearing the canyon ridge. The waters had become unusually quiet and in the moonlight, he spotted a tiny beach by the receding canyon edge.

Could he beach the dugout for the rest of the night? But no! There were tigers in those forests that covered the canyon and they came down to drink at night. He tried to laugh again but only a hoarse gurgle came out of his throat. Persistent, he pushed closer to the shore without touching it and there were night jungle sounds - sleepy birds murmuring and quarrelsome monkeys on the prowl. So to keep awake he amused himself with his new found treasure - a sound in his throat. He practiced voicing their calls and was fascinated when they returned them, till no longer caring for tigers, angry men or rainbows, he fell asleep in a crumpled huddle on the floor of the boat.

Hours later and in daylight, he awoke and found himself and his dugout in an eerie place. The river had spread to an almost silent lagoon. It was so quiet and yet there was a distant roaring of water in the far away. It was something not known to him and he felt a lurking danger. Above him, the towering cliffs on either side were so close they seemed as if they would stop the water and the roaring must be them quarreling over whether or not they would let the river pass. He pulled his dugout onto the patches of sands nearby and wondered. He would have to climb those cliffs and look down on his new world before venturing further.

He cut some banana fronds into strips and wove them into a rope and then tied his boat to a tree. Completely naked without even a breechcloth and with the broken knife between his teeth, he carefully and cautiously climbed the cliff to the top and looked with awe and bewilderment at the scene beneath. It was such a narrow gorge and so full of raging water that it sent up a spray and soaked his naked body. The river and the gorge were indeed at war with each other. His boat would never make it, at least not with himself in it. Below was such hurling foam that he could scarcely see the water.

He looked faraway in the distance beyond and thought he could see some sort of living place a long way off. But how was he to get there?

He climbed down slowly, sometimes having to drop a sheer ten feet into rough gorse and ever fearful of tigers, carefully made his way to his dugout, patiently waiting for him on the sandy strip. Perhaps, it would make it by itself and perhaps also, it would be battered into driftwood. He himself, would scale the cliff again and make his way along the shore, if there were one, and search to see if his boat had passed through the canyon. And what would happen to him there? He was naked and without words. He sadly untied his dugout and pushed it into mid-stream and watched while it was sucked into the gorge.

He did not feel like trying to laugh. He just thought a message: 'Goodbye, my friend. And safe passage.'

He climbed the canyon wall again, the jagged outcrops tearing his hands and then picked a way along the top and down the other side looking all the time at the furious waters beneath where his boat must surely have disappeared because nothing could survive in that raging torrent. And all the while he thought a silent prayer: 'River, my river, take me to your home.'

He walked for two days, eating dead fish thrown up on the riverside. The river seemed quieter now, broader and more silent. He searched for his boat along the way but there was nothing but driftwood torn from the mountain trees further upstream. He saw no one but a few peasant farmers who were friendly enough and seemed to ask in a language unknown to him where he was going. Since he couldn't reply and was without any clothes at all, they shrugged and passed by. Just another wild jungle boy, they probably thought.

He never went far from his river and it seemed to sing to him - come with me, come with me - in a now more restful voice.

He collected some more banana fronds and sitting by the river, he plaited himself a loincloth. If there were people then, there must be a village nearby. What sort of village, he asked himself, as he wove not only a clout but a shepherd's cloak as well, then looked at himself in the quiet pools along the river. He thought he looked rather well in the green reflection on the river and he tried to utter a sound but it only came out like a birdcall. And then he was afraid to seek out the village. He would be laughed at and perhaps people would chase him out or run at the sight of him. They might think he was an evil spirit sent to do them harm. People seemed to be like that everywhere unless you were the same as they were. Perhaps he WAS a spirit - a spirit of the river. For Khan didn't really know what he was except that he was different from other people.

Still hesitant, he lingered by the river and one day, cut a reed and fashioned it into a music pipe like he'd seen boys do in his village. He breathed carefully into it and the sound that came out was the music of the river; the rushing waters, the quiet ripples, the winds and even the roar of the canyon and the voices of the birds in the forest.

Khan was delighted with himself and spent two whole days with his new toy forgetting he was hungry and that it was dangerous to sleep by the river. It was much warmer here than in his village and he had heard that there were strange animals in the waters downstream; water pythons, hippos and crocodiles, although he himself had never seen them.

It was hunger that finally drove him from the river's marshy bank. He had to venture into the village and into the market and it was late afternoon when he finally arrived there.

It was an uncommon one for him and much larger and dirtier than his own or even the last one he had strayed into. Not quaintly curious like the last one, but completely unfamiliar and bizarre. He gawked and stared while busy people pushed him aside from standing in the pathway. And all over, there were strange boxes that made loud music and blared all the time till he wondered how they could hear their own chatter; many fruits and sweet cakes he had never seen in his short life; a large box on rubber wheels that emptied and got full again of people all the time who shrieked and shouted in another calling language he had never heard; stalls of bright clothes and little round hats that all the men and boys wore in his own village. But their speaking was different. Khan had crossed another border.

Terrified, he stood at the edge of the market and looked and gaped and nobody paid him any attention. There were so many curiously dressed men, women and children running in all directions. Refuse was thrown here and there and everywhere. Naked children played in the slimy gutters and around the stalls and were cuffed off occasionally but never really went very far away. He went to one of the filthy streams running from the stalls and full of discarded fruits and peeling and picked up one he'd never seen before. It was soft and pink on the inside and green and hard on the outside. He ate it all and it was like a cool drink of water but soon gave him a pain in his belly as the thick peels were not for eating and especially not when his stomach was empty.

Soon a boorish bunch of boys crowded around him and seemed to be curious of his strange appearance and rudely asked him where he came from - apparently, because he did not understand their voices. They were ragged and dirty and had on bits of clothing he had sometimes seen on boys whose fathers came and went on the dock boats. When he didn't reply they laughed and pointed at him and pushed him further into the gutter stream. To ignore them and because he was scared, he pulled out his flute and played but again came his wild animal and bird and river calls and they laughed all the more but it was not like his own laughter. It was crude, hostile laughter and they crowded nearer and tried to take his flute till they were roughly pushed aside by a large and very differently clothed man. Khan had noticed him watching from a distance. He was not dressed in any kind of clothes he had ever seen before and his face was so pale and he had light coloured hair.

Now Khan had made a very appealing picture sitting beside the littered stream in his woven loin cloth and shepherd cloak while playing his flute. He was a handsome boy and his black hair now reached his shoulders and his expressive dark eyes revealed his sadness and his hunger. He continued playing his music not daring to look very far beyond himself.

The stranger quickly held up a small black box with round glassy eyes and he heard a snap like a dry reed breaking. He was frightened and wanted to run away but found he couldn't move. Then the rude rabble crowded around the strange man shouting for him to do the same to them and crying - one rupee! One rupee! And Khan thought this must be a very rich market if beggars can ask for one rupee. He himself had never seen a rupee.

The man shoved them off and holding out his hand urged Khan to follow him. But Khan shook his head till the man took his hand and pulled him to his feet. They went together to the market and stopped at a stall where a woman was selling cooked rice and curry and fruit. Khan's eyes widened with the sight. The man gestured to him to sit down on the ground around the charcoal brazier and then spoke to the woman in what must have been her own language. She immediately spooned out a large portion of rice and sauce onto a banana leaf and handed it to Khan. The man tried again to speak to him but he just shook his head and put his hands to his throat and then sat silently fingering the food to his mouth. When he finished, he folded the leaf and tucked it into his loin strip to savor later. In the meantime, the stranger had given the woman a handful of coins and pointing to the timepiece on his wrist, had gone away.

So Khan rose and bowed to the woman and turned to leave. No! No! She seemed to say while pointing to the ground where he had sat cross-legged by the cooking pot. He shook his head again with one hand across his chest. Then she gestured with a finger to come back and pointed to her timepiece on her wrist. She must be very rich indeed to have a time-teller, and the man too, as he had given her money for the food. He hesitated and then nodded a reply.

What did they want of him, he wondered, a boy with no clothes but plaited reeds and no voice and no possessions but a reed flute and a broken knife? He disappeared with the shadows of the swift tropical evening and finding an empty stall table further up the street, crept under it to sleep for the night. The babble of people seemed to have all gone away as suddenly as the daylight. He lay there and considered and thought he would go back to the woman again in the morning.

He awoke to a thudding on the tabletop above him. The shopkeeper was setting out his wares and he would have to go and go quickly. He waited till he saw his bare brown legs disappearing into his shop. But soon there were many other smaller legs crowding around the table and then running down the street. He recognized the voices of the rough crowd who had pestered him the day before. The merchant came running out of his shop. Dazed and scared, Khan crept from under the table. The shopkeeper had already caught two of the boys and was beating them but they quickly pointed to Khan and everyone shouted and shrieked and protested in that language he didn't understand.

He fled down the street with hordes of people chasing him; the rough young louts of yesterday and men with sticks and whips, past the woman's stall where she was already cooking rice cakes where the stranger had befriended him, past the slimy riverlet where he had sat and played his flute and been tormented, past donkey and peasants entering the market. He ran and ran not knowing where he was going till he realized he had outrun them all and was nearing the river.

He lost himself in the marshy reeds and not caring about his stomach pains or river pythons or anything at all crouched there for hours. It was past noon when he pulled aside the marsh grass to wonder where he could be. The river was silent and being the heat of the day, so were the birds asleep. He soon knew he was further downstream. The river was running slowly, ever so slowly and it was so hot.

'River, my river, where are we going? Where is your home?' but the river didn't reply. It moved listlessly like an old man. Perhaps it was thinking or dreaming till sundown.

Khan stopped suddenly. He had heard a voice strangely like the voices of his own village. He looked around and saw no one. Was it himself then? His own self speaking? He repeated his question and the river replied: soon, soon! And Khan lay in the marshy edge and laughed and laughed and the laughter was good for his throat. It became louder and louder and sometimes sounded like the river rippling over the rocks in his village.

He walked for several days closely following the river edge and talked aloud to himself all the way. He often thought of the stranger who had bought him some food and the woman who had tapped her timekeeper wanting him to return. Should he go back and try to find them?

But no. He was frightened and had had enough of unfamiliar villages and angry people. For sure the shopkeeper would get him by recognizing him in his strange clothing and he had no others. He even avoided the road that ran some way back from the river.

It was nearing evening when he noticed that now, the tired old river was parting company with itself. It was creeping slowly into many smaller rivers and soon Khan found himself walking on a long sand bar. He followed it for miles till it ended and there before him was a large river - so large it had no banks at all. So this was the river's home? It had joined hands with a river much larger than it had ever been.

The waters around and before him seemed so silent and peaceful. But it was the end of his river. Khan could go no further. With his feet soothing in the warm brackish water, he took out his flute and answered the raucous voices of the large white birds swooping around and above him. Then he lay back on the warm sand and laughed again - not so loudly this time as his body was wasted with fatigue and hunger. But it was so good to laugh, even feebly. He had outwitted them all but where was he to go since he could go no further without his friend, the river? He could never find his way back home and here the sand was warm beneath him. Perhaps he would go and live in the forests since he could sound the voices of the wild animals. There was fruit in the forests and he could hunt and carve. Drowsily he fingered the broken blade of his knife in the loincloth. He could even build himself a house and perhaps he would find his rainbow again. But Khan was already asleep with such a deep sleep and being a village boy from beyond was not aware of the creeping, treacherous tides already seeping in from the Bay of Bengal.

Shama Books
Addis Ababa
www.shamabooks.com